CHARADE BOOK THREE

THE

TRUTH

paige press

CHARADE BOOK THREE

THE TRUTH

STELLA GRAY

Paige Press
Leander, TX 78641

Ebook:
ISBN: 978-1-953520-52-4

Print:
ISBN: 978-1-953520-53-1

Editing: Erica Russikoff at Erica Edits
Proofing: Michele Ficht

Broken Bride

Broken Vow

Broken Trust

ABOUT THIS BOOK

My family has given everything to salvage the Zoric name and reputation from my father's tarnished legacy.

I only needed a moment to destroy it all.

Along with two hearts.

It was supposed to be a simple charade. I never thought Ford and I would fall in love.

But I can't take back what I've done.

He can't change the past.

And what we've done changes everything.

But only if I stop running.

Someone has to lose either way. But when the truth comes out, it might just be all of us.

PROLOGUE

FORD

The sun was shining down on the verdant, perfectly landscaped quad at Wayland-Blaine Academy. Birds were chirping, the memorial fountain was splashing, and privileged students with no clue what the real world was like were frolicking around in their freshly dry-cleaned uniforms like the assholes they were.

I was so done with this place.

Two girls walked by with binders clutched to their chests, laughing with each other. Other kids sprawled under shady oaks in their stupid cliques eating lunch. Everybody was oblivious, just going about their days as if their lives hadn't just imploded. Unlike me.

This never would have happened if I hadn't left my chemistry textbook at home. Normally I didn't lug it back and forth to school—the thing weighed at least five pounds —but we had a test today, and because the price of tuition granted us certain *considerations*, it was going to be open-book. Being a fairly average student, my GPA needed all the help it could get. Hence my mad dash home after third period.

But now all I could think about was how much I wished I'd remembered the fucking book when I had left for school this morning, instead of having to sneak back into my own house and accidentally overhearing my parents having another one of their arguments.

At least, that's what I'd thought it was. Until I heard what they were actually saying.

My parents fought plenty, but always about small stuff. Where to go for dinner. Who to invite to parties. To whom they were or were not speaking in their social circle. The usual.

This argument had been different. I could tell from the moment I heard the tone of my mother's voice that it was something serious. Serious like cancer, or a death in the family, or some kind of catastrophic financial or (God forbid) social ruin. Which is why I'd decided to eavesdrop.

I should have walked away.

But there's a reason they say curiosity killed the cat.

"You're disgusting," my mother was saying as I crept toward the library doors.

"Stop being so melodramatic," Dad had replied, sounding bored. "It's an open secret. You think I'm the only one doing it?"

"These dalliances aren't just a stain on our marriage. They're embarrassing. You promised you'd stop!"

I was shocked to hear the tears in her voice; she wasn't the emotional type. In fact, I'd never seen my mother cry. Usually if she got upset about something, she simply left the room. Which meant she might come barreling out the door any moment. I ducked behind the heavy drapes and held my breath.

That was when the rest of it fully sank in. *Dalliances.* Plural. My father had been having an affair—no, multiple affairs. He'd been stepping out behind my mom's back, and apparently after he'd made a vow to stop. Meaning he had a history of cheating.

I'd had no idea.

Sure, I knew my parents didn't have a warm, cutesy marriage like the kind I saw on TV, but I still thought they had a stable relationship. One that was solid and built on mutual respect and compatibility, if not affection.

My mother wasn't done talking.

"Ever since you got mixed up with Konstantin Zoric, it's been one 'rumor' after another," she hissed. "And I know they're not just rumors. Some of those girls are barely eighteen."

She was definitely crying. My stomach churned. Dad was screwing Konstantin's models?

Zoric...the name was familiar. Not just because Konstantin ran KZ Modeling, which was one of the most famous agencies in the world, but because his kids were classmates of mine at Wayland-Blaine. Stefan had graduated already, though he was still kind of a legend, but Luka was a senior this year and then the youngest one was Mary, or Maureen...no, Mara. I never paid much attention to her— she was kind of a quiet, lone wolf type—and even though she was pretty enough, there were plenty of other girls at school to keep me occupied.

"They're not affairs, dear," I heard my father say drolly. "Not technically."

"Not *technically*? What does that mean?" My mother's voice was shrill and panicked.

"They're paid," he said. "It's transactional. Not a real relationship. Don't take it so personally."

3

"They're hookers? And that's supposed to make me feel better?"

I stood there, frozen in shock. Not only had my father been cheating, long term, but he was doing it with *sex workers* supplied by my classmate's father. Actual prostitutes. No wonder my mother was freaking out. Talk about adding insult to injury.

Mom had let out another pathetic wail, and that's when I'd slipped down the hall and out the front door. I couldn't listen to any more of that. They had to be on the brink of divorce. And I'd seen divorce rip through families before.

My friends with divorced parents had gotten uprooted, their entire lives thrown into disarray. Everything had changed. They had shared custody arrangements, different homes, different sets of rules, parents who continued to bicker and snipe at each other from afar. Some of my friends had even been forced to move away from Chicago to live in the fucking burbs, or even out of state. Others only saw their mom or dad on the weekend, or during school breaks.

That kind of change to my life, my routine, would be the worst thing on the planet. Not just disruptive, but humiliating. And what if the lawyer fees or the divorce settlement or my mom's alimony messed with my allowance? What if I had to give up my car?

The whole drive back to campus, I was in a rage.

So here I was, brooding during the remainder of my lunch period, gripping my book so hard my fingers had gone numb.

My life as I knew it was over.

Mainly, I was furious at my father. Obviously. How hard was it to keep your dick in your pants when you were that old? But my mom was to blame, too. The way she nagged and shopped her way through the money in their checking account every month and generally made herself a royal pain to be around, it was no wonder Dad had been driven to seek out other women. My mother prided herself on being the ideal society wife—going to the right events, always looking perfectly put together no matter what, making sure she was seen with and by the right people—but behind closed doors, it was a whole other story.

I hated to think about it in detail, but it was clear she fucked up whatever her wifely duties to my father were supposed to be. When a man was getting what he needed from his marriage, he had no reason to wander, be it for emotional or physical reasons.

Regardless of the state of their relationship, though, I didn't want them to get a divorce. Why should I have to suffer just because they'd made poor choices? They said the vows, 'til death do they part, and as far as I was concerned that meant they should stay married. For my sake, at least. They could separate after I left for college. It was only a few more years.

Gripping my Mountain Dew can had left me with a fist full of crumpled aluminum. As I walked over to the recycling can, I debated just leaving campus. Playing hooky for the rest of the day. Maybe I'd hit up one of the dive bars on Lincoln Ave that wouldn't look too hard at my fake ID.

Then I saw Mara Zoric walking across the quad.

Konstantin Zoric's daughter.

He was the person who was really to blame for all of this. My father would have never gotten involved with a revolving door of barely legal sex workers if it wasn't for that scumbaggy piece of shit and his so-called "modeling agency," which was clearly just a front for prostitutes. And meanwhile I'd have to see Mara at school every day, watching her sashay around without a care in the world, as though her father hadn't singlehandedly just ruined my life and the lives of countless others.

It didn't help that she was prettier than I'd realized, which somehow made it all worse. That long black hair, the heart-shaped face, the kind of tits you just can't hide. She was usually the wallflower type, but I could see her laughing with someone at the other end of the quad.

My vision went red.

Suddenly, all I wanted was for her to feel as bad as I did right now. Like her whole world was falling apart, and couldn't ever be put back together. I wondered if she knew what her father really did. What paid for her nice house, her private school tuition, the black town car that dropped her off every day. I mean, the girl wasn't stupid. She probably knew everything.

I had a Sharpie in my backpack.

Ducking back into the building, I stalked to the main hallway, to the row of lockers that faced the front entrance doors of the school. Those lockers were the first thing you saw when you walked in every morning, flanked on both sides by gleaming trophy cases, the Wayland-Blaine crest hanging on a banner above.

I glanced down the hall to make sure it was empty. Everyone was either at lunch or in their afternoon classes. I knew it didn't matter which locker I wrote on.

In big, black, capital letters, I wrote Mara's name. Her full name: MARA ZORIC. Then underneath it, IS A WHORE.

The janitor would clean it up soon enough, but that

didn't matter. All that mattered was that everyone in school would see it first. The rumor mill would do the rest.

Sharpie in hand, I turned toward the gym. My revenge was far from complete. Next stop: the boys' locker room.

FORD

CHAPTER 1

Against all odds, See Yourself's fundraising event at the Four Seasons was turning out to be a huge success.

The Grand Ballroom was packed, the mood sophisticated without being stuffy. Emzee was going to raise a ton for her charity and I couldn't be happier for her. Despite the snafus we had encountered during the planning process, the last-minute catering and sound system issues that cropped up earlier today, and the fact that my ex Claudia had barely managed to do her job, the event had gone off without a hitch thus far.

Yet somehow, nothing was turning out the way I thought it would. Not with the event, of course—surveying the tables, all I saw were happy faces and raised flutes of champagne, which meant people were going to be writing some pretty big checks before they left—but there was definitely something going on with Emzee. I'd barely seen my wife since we arrived. In fact, it almost felt like she was avoiding me.

This should have been our triumphant debut, but

whenever I managed to catch a glimpse of her mingling with the guests, I could tell that her smile was forced. Was it just her anxiety? I knew crowds made her uncomfortable, but at the same time, shouldn't some of the stress that had been dogging her leading up to this night be gone now? Her big event was finally happening, and happening well. If there was a time to celebrate her accomplishments, this was it. But every time I started toward her, she'd disappear back into the fray.

"Ah, young Ford Malone, there you are!"

I turned to find Nathan Watson—a real estate developer and old friend of my father—standing behind me with a plate of canapés. He pulled me into a half hug with his free arm.

"Good to see you, Mr. Watson," I coughed out as he slapped me heartily on the back.

"Pleasure's all mine," he said, brandishing his plate. "Quail egg on toast?"

I waved it away. "Oh, no thank you. Afraid I overindulged on smoked oysters already."

"Rookie move! You've got to save room to try them all," he said with a laugh. "Figured with the hefty dona-tion I'm making, I might as well eat my weight in puff pastries."

"My wife will be pleased on both counts," I told him, straightening my rumpled tux. "Speaking of which, I was just about to go find her."

"I saw her over by the orchestra a moment ago," he said.

Looking across the room, I thought I could see the top of her head. She was so short, it was hard to tell, though. "Thanks for the tip, sir. Enjoy your evening."

With that, I glided away. It's not that I wasn't a well-trained master in the art of idle chitchat with bougie types, but Emzee's vanishing act was giving me my own case of anxiety.

As I ducked around trays of champagne and onion tarts and pricy cheeses and pâté, I suddenly realized that she was possibly still jealous about Claudia's involvement in the fundraiser, and my ex's recent failed attempts to woo me back.

Could it be? Even after what happened with my parents in the library earlier, when I'd walked in on them trying to blackmail her and break up our marriage? I'd rushed into the room to defend Em, and then the two of us had fucked in a frenzy in the guest room afterward, which I had to admit was actually probably what people referred to as making love. Because, yeah. We'd both said the words. Fully recommitted to each other with our bodies and our pledge to stay together. For the first time, it had seemed like our marital vow to become one was finally real.

Even before that, I'd been convinced that our relationship was on the mend after I flew to New York to get Emzee back from a conference she'd jetted off to. It had seemed like a turning point for us. I'd done my best ever since to sweep her off her feet, to show her that even if our relationship had started out as a legal arrangement, we could make it a real marriage.

Did she still not get it? It was the two of us against the world—and it always would be. As for Claudia, she would always fall into the "world" category.

Hovering at the edge of the platform where the five-piece orchestra played classy versions of Top 40 pop hits, I scanned the room once again. Where the hell was she? I went over to the bar and tried texting her one more time, but either she wasn't looking at her phone (likely) or she was purposely ignoring my texts. Fuck.

All I wanted was to steal her away to a corner, pour her a glass of champagne, and toast to a successful evening. And at the end of the night I'd take her home, strip her out of that sexy dress, and reward her for all of her hard work. Reward her over and over and over again. I couldn't get enough of her. How responsive she was to my touch. How she knew exactly what I wanted and was eager to give it to me. That's how I wanted this evening to wrap up. But for now, I couldn't even manage to get near her. My ex, on the other hand—I'd spent most of the night trying to avoid her. Every time I turned around, she was making eyes at me. With her huge blue ballgown and that blown-out blonde mane, she was impossible to miss.

"*Ford*," a voice purred from behind me.

Speak of the devil.

"Claudia," I said, turning around with a whiskey in hand. "Enjoying yourself?"

"Immensely." She put her talon-like nails on my shoulders, using them to keep me in place while she forced a lingering double cheek kiss. I did all I could to not push her away. She was being ridiculous, per usual, but I wasn't about to cause a scene.

"You're welcome, by the way," Claudia said, gesturing around the room like a magician showing off a rabbit fresh out of a hat.

She was flushed with pride, and even though I was annoyed at her, I couldn't blame her for feeling like she'd done a good job. She'd taken us to tour all the best venues in town, had used her relationships to get us a great deal, and even if she'd been less than helpful today, she'd still managed to put together a great event in service of Emzee's charity. I was grateful for that.

"Thank you," I told her, easing her hand off my shoulder. "Everything turned out perfectly."

"I know," she said with a satisfied grin. "Where's wifey, by the way?"

The flirtatious gleam in her eyes didn't fade, which immediately made me suspicious that she was responsible for Emzee's distance somehow.

"It's funny. Now that you mention it, something *has* been up with her tonight. You know anything about that?" I doubted I'd get a straight answer out of Claudia, but it was worth a try.

"Maybe it's her period. How would I know?"

I gave her a look, and she gave me an irritated raise of her brows. Clearly this conversation wasn't going the way she was expecting.

"I saw you walk out of the guest bathroom right before her back at my parents' house, and she's been acting off ever since," I pointed out. "What happened?"

She flashed me an inelegant eye roll. "Is it against the law for two women to use the same bathroom? Seriously, stop trying to pin this on me. I have nothing to do with your marital woes."

My drink was empty, my adrenaline was pumping, and my intuition was telling me that my ex was full of shit. "You said something to her."

"What on Earth, Ford? You're the one who left her behind to go out for drinks with me, remember? Take some responsibility. And by the way, I seem to recall that when you and I were together, we simply communicated our problems and then worked through them. Like adults."

Smiling sourly, I said, "Look how good that worked out for us. There are some things you just can't fix, Claudia."

Such as the fact that she was a selfish, petty, self-centered social climber. That she had wanted to be with me not because of me, but because of how good we looked together. How well-matched our family wealth was. How compatible our elite social circles were.

It had taken me a long time to realize that I didn't want what Claudia had to offer at all.

The kind of person I wanted dedicated her time and effort to helping other people. She was whip smart and sexy and sweet and she had always liked me for me. Or at least, the person I tried to be. Emzee made me want to be a better person.

"Whatever," Claudia said. "All I'm saying is, maybe you weren't ready for marriage. Maybe *she* wasn't."

I didn't like the look in her eyes. It was one I'd seen before. Whenever she had a secret or some good gossip and was just waiting for it to explode so she could watch the ugly aftermath. Of course, she was usually the one who did something to make it explode.

"You are the last person," I told her, leaning in close, "that I need relationship advice from. Last time I checked, you were still single."

Her eyes widened, and I knew I'd hit a nerve.

With a huff, she spun on her stiletto and flounced away. Good riddance.

I got a fresh drink and circled the room again, to no avail. As much as I hated to admit it, what Claudia had said —about me and Emzee not being ready for marriage—did make sense. How could it not? We'd gotten married basically on a whim. My whim. I'd coerced her into marrying me temporarily, just to piss my parents off and keep them off my back about the whole getting-back-together-with-Claudia nonsense. Not that Claudia (or anyone else) knew that.

And yeah, Emzee had been resistant from the beginning. I'd blamed her hesitation on a dozen things, but I'd never considered that she wasn't actually ready to be married. Especially since I was the groom. It was no secret that she'd been in love with me since high school.

Then again, it was obvious she had a lot of trust issues when it came to relationships. She'd never been in a long-term one before. In fact, our seven-year friendship was probably the longest non-family relationship that Emzee had ever had. Of course I'd done nothing but take advantage of it, since day one.

My gut twisted.

Maybe I'd moved too fast with all that Love Talk earlier today. Maybe it was too much, too soon. Maybe it was too much to ask of a girl with all her trust issues, assuming she'd simply drop them just because I defended her to my parents.

I probably just needed to give her some time to process. Between my declaration of love and the fight with my parents and the fundraiser, she had to be feeling completely overwhelmed.

Suddenly, I realized that it was the first time I'd come to her defense because I wanted to, and not out of guilt over what had happened to her in high school.

Not that she could ever know what really happened back then.

Now *that* would ruin everything.

FORD

CHAPTER 2

"What an incredible night, huh?" I said, reaching my arm around Emzee to rub her shoulder.

It was almost midnight. After the fundraiser had finally wound down, we'd dealt with some administrative tasks and now we stood outside waiting for the car service to arrive.

"Mm," she replied, edging out of my grasp.

So she was still upset. And at this point, it seemed unlikely it had anything do with the event. It was something to do with me. Great.

At least we were headed home. I had never in my life been so glad for a party to end. Back in my single days, I would have been gearing up for the after-party, not wanting the evening to end, happy to just keep the drinks flowing and have a good time with my friends.

That was all behind me. Married life had made me a homebody. Well, not just that. It was Emzee specifically. She'd taught me to appreciate a night in, taught me the true meaning of Netflix and chill in the most literal sense, and yeah, I was excited to see Munchkin after work so he could attack me with slobbery French bulldog kisses. But I had no idea what would happen once we got back to the apartment tonight. If my wife would have a conversation with me, or even be willing to sleep in the same room.

I'd barely gotten a moment alone with her all evening, which I'd convinced myself was the result of her being in such high demand. She'd done amazingly well, just as I knew she would. Working her magic, schmoozing with potential donors, charming their damn socks off and getting those wallets open. See Yourself had already earned money from the fundraiser tickets, of course, but the organization was going to reap the benefits of this night long term, thanks to the fact that it had shined a bright, positive light on the charity and welcomed a whole new batch of donors to the fold. And it was all because of Emzee's passion and hard work.

"Did you get a chance to talk to the reporter from the *Tribune*?" I asked, trying to warm her up. "She was pretty impressed by See Yourself's mission statement. I saw her making the rounds and chatting up the guests, but she told me she wanted to interview you too."

"We spoke," Emzee said, not even turning in my direction.

"I'm sure it went well. What about the guy taking notes for the *Sun-Times* and whomever the *Daily Herald* sent?"

Whirling toward me, Emzee glared. "Yes, Ford, I chatted up every single guest, rubbed every last elbow, and met every fucking obligation that I had tonight. Claudia certainly covered all the PR bases with her invitations. Maybe *she's* the one you should be congratulating."

Frowning, I said, "It's your charity, Em, and this was your event. I'm congratulating *you*. Why are you pissed at me? What did I do?"

She scowled. "You know what you did. And you thought you could get away with it."

"Can you just tell me how I fucked up, so I can apologize? You've barely said two words to me since we got here, and every time you look at me I see daggers in your eyes."

It was true. Even now, I was getting nothing but pure loathing from her expression.

Of course that was the exact moment our town car rolled up.

"Good evening, Mr. and Mrs. Malone," the driver said, climbing out to open the back door for us.

Emzee nodded at him and slid into the back seat. I followed after her. By the time I was settled, my wife already had her back to me, eyes glued to her cell phone.

"Em?" I said, speaking softly.

"No," she snapped. "Just don't."

I was at a loss. Despite my earlier fears, her attitude didn't seem to have anything to do with the possible overwhelm of us embarking on the rest of our lives together as a couple. This seemed like...pure anger. What did I do?

Sighing, I loosened my bow tie and shrugged out of my suit jacket.

Retracing my steps following our quickie in the guest room at my parents' place, I racked my brain trying to remember what I could have done or said to mess things up, some misstep I must have taken during the gala. Did I inadvertently insult a big name donor? Impossible. I'd been going to events like this since I was a kid. I knew how to act around these kinds of people.

Had I given Emzee the impression that I'd been flirting with other women? If so, it would only have been out of professional cordiality, to encourage more donations—no other woman could catch my attention these days. I was sure my wife knew that.

And sure, Claudia had been eye-fucking me all night, but that wasn't my fault. I hadn't encouraged it. Even if Emzee had caught sight of Claudia putting her hands on me, she would have also seen how quickly I brushed off my ex's advances.

We were already halfway home. My place in Streeterville was barely a mile from the Four Seasons. The last thing I wanted was for us to go to bed angry once we got there.

"Please talk to me," I tried again, but she didn't look up from her phone. "Whatever it is, I can't fix it if I don't know what I did wrong."

Tucking her phone into her bag, she glanced up at the privacy window separating us from the driver and seemed to realize that we were alone for the first time this evening.

"Actually, I've got a question for you," she said, sliding closer to me, eyes narrowing.

"Okay. Shoot."

"Do you remember our sophomore year at Wayland-Blaine? The year we met?"

Suddenly I was uneasy. "Yeah..."

"Who wrote that I was a whore on all the lockers? Who started all those rumors about me? Do you know anything about that, Ford? Hmm?"

The world dropped out from under me. How the hell did she find out about—

And then I realized exactly how. Of course.

Fucking Claudia.

I knew she was involved somehow. That explained her satisfied little grin. Her smug comments. Her marriage advice.

I was furious at Claudia, but I'd deal with her later. Right now, I needed to make things right with my wife. "Look, I can explain."

"*You*," she said, her voice full of disgust. "You're the one who started all the rumors. Why? Just so you could be the one to save me from them? Do you have any idea how fucked up that is? Or what it feels like to know our entire relationship is based on a lie?"

My stomach churned. "But that was..." I started, then shook my head. "It was a long time ago, and you don't have the full story—"

"I don't need any more of your stories!" she cut me off. "I've had enough of them. Of you. So just stop." She turned back toward the window, dismissing me like I barely mattered.

"There was more to it," I insisted, feeling sick.

Glancing over, Emzee hissed, "Really? Like what? That you knew about my father's 'other business' back then?"

My mouth opened, and then closed. How could I even begin to answer that?

"Well?" Emzee prodded. "Did you?"

Fuck.

I didn't think the situation could get any worse, that there could be anything more damaging than confessing that yes, I'd been the one to graffiti the locker room back at the academy and start the rumors about Emzee being a whore. But admitting that I'd known about her father's sex trafficking ring all those years ago would hurt her even more.

So I didn't answer her.

Unfortunately, my lack of response only confirmed for Emzee what she already knew.

Blinking back tears, she let out a hollow laugh. "You did

know. All that time I was in the dark about my dad and the KZ models, *you knew*. Seven years we were friends, Ford, and you knew the *entire time*. And you kept it all a secret. You kept both of your secrets."

"Wait. You need to understand," I said, knowing I sounded desperate. "Things were different back then. *I* was different back then. I'm not the same kid I was in high school."

She looked at me and I waited for that spark, for that sign of affection that I always saw in her eyes. That indication that I was still her hero, even after all of this.

But there was nothing there but pain, anger, and betrayal.

"No," she said. "Back then you were a shitty kid."

Her words felt like a knife in my chest. Then she continued, twisting it even deeper.

"Now, you're just a bad person."

Our car had pulled up to the curb outside my building, but when the driver came around to open the car door, she didn't move to get out. Instead, she crossed her arms.

"Emzee, let's go upstairs. I'll make you tea, and we can sit and talk it out."

She shook her head. "I'm not going anywhere with you. I'm going to Stefan's. Now get the hell out."

EMZEE

CHAPTER 3

ike I always say, there's nothing like an emergency girls' night to prop you up when you find out your husband is a lying, backstabbing, manipulative asshole and your entire world is shattered beyond repair. Or something like that.

Thank God Tori had agreed to dog sit Munchkin during the fundraiser.

His warm, burly little body in my arms and the dark chocolate gelato in my hands were just about the only things keeping me in one piece. Tori and I were on the couch with our feet up, a blanket draped over our laps. I swiped at my leaking eyes with the sleeve of the oversized sweatshirt she had loaned me and took another bite of gelato, but the taste was bittersweet.

"I'm so sorry, Em," Tori said, already scraping the bottom of her pint of salted caramel.

All I could do was nod.

Even though I'd known in my gut that Claudia had been right about Ford's involvement in my high school torment and his knowledge of my father's secret business, it had still been a shock when Ford refused to deny it. Some part of me had been holding on to the futile hope that Claudia had been lying...but seeing the way Ford's face had fallen when I called him out in the car had made me want to throw up. Or maybe that was just morning sickness. In the evening.

"I don't get why he did it in the first place, though it's easy enough to chalk it up to sixteen-year-old Ford Malone dickishness," I mused. "But I still don't understand why he went through the charade of rescuing me from the bullies afterward, and then faking a friendship with me for the last seven years. The whole thing is just...kind of sociopathic."

Tori frowned. "What makes you think the friendship was fake?"

"Uh, the fact that he never told me the truth? He's been lying this whole time. By omission."

She shook her head. "That doesn't mean you weren't friends. It just means he was covering his ass. Obviously he knew you'd be pissed at him if you found out. Maybe pissed enough not to be his friend anymore. Right? I mean, you guys are—were—best friends."

"Maybe. Or maybe he was just using me all along. Or fucking with me for his own amusement. I was like his puppet. What did Claudia say I was...his 'little sucker fish.'"

"That bitch," Tori said, which was pretty spicy for her. My other sister-in-law, Brooklyn, was usually the resident trash talker. And I loved her for it.

It was almost one in the morning. Thankfully, my brother hadn't even blinked when I showed up on his doorstep after the gala. I'd texted on the way over and was greeted warmly by Stefan, Tori, and the only man in my life who was still completely loyal to me—Munchkin.

With a groan of effort, Tori leaned forward to set her

empty gelato container on the coffee table, but her huge belly was in the way.

"Let me do that," I said, grabbing the container from her. "You just take it easy. The last thing we need is you going into early labor from overexerting yourself."

She laughed. "I highly doubt that leaning over is going to do that."

"You can't be too safe when it comes to my niece," I teased, though under the blanket, I reflexively put my hand on my still-flat stomach.

Every time I glanced at Tori's bump, I was reminded about the secret I myself was carrying—literally. The uncertainty of my future was a million times scarier knowing that I didn't only carry the burden of the Zoric family's debt on my shoulders, but that there was an innocent life involved now, too. An innocent life that was forbidden to even exist, under the terms set by Ford's parents. After all, they had stipulated that I was not to get pregnant, and I had to obey if I wanted them to keep their end of the bargain and pay off the Russian mob.

That meant the baby had to be a secret. From everyone. Especially Ford.

But this tiny spark inside me...I'd do anything to protect it. That meant I had to come up with a plan, and fast. Unfortunately, all I could manage to do at the moment was cry into my gelato as a fresh wave of tears hit me. Munchkin wriggled in my arms, attacking my chin with slobbery licks.

Tori patted my arm. "Love is easy. But marriage is hard. Especially when someone's been keeping a secret. Speaking from experience, though, it doesn't mean it's all over."

"Yeah, but..." I shook my head. "I don't know if I want it to be over or not. Maybe I can't forgive him."

"Give it a little time," Tori said. "Your wounds are fresh.

And you're welcome to stay with us as long as you need. Munchkin, too. Stefan put fresh sheets on the guest bed for you."

"You two are the best."

Sighing, I rested my head on her shoulder and stared at the TV. I wasn't even sure what was on, but it was some kind of home renovation show.

"I'm sorry for keeping you up so late, Tor. I'm sure you're exhausted."

"Oh, don't worry about it. I slept for almost four hours right before dinner, so I'm actually wide awake. Hence my HGTV marathoning. My sleep schedule has been totally screwy. It's so hard to get comfortable."

"I guess it'll be good practice for when the baby comes," I said.

"Honestly, I can't wait. I feel like my body's been taken hostage."

I laughed. "I'm not sure I've ever heard anyone describe being pregnant that way."

"That came out wrong," Tori said, laughing with me. "It's not that I'm not super excited about the baby, and I'm grateful that we get to build a family. It's just...it's a lot."

"How does it feel?" I asked, nodding toward her belly. "What's it like?"

She let out a groan, putting her feet up on the coffee table.

"It's not all morning sickness and insomnia and swollen feet and back pain, but that's definitely part of it," she admitted. "My body has changed so much, and it's taken a lot of getting used to. I never thought I'd have a kid so young. But...I don't think it was real to me until I could feel her kicking in there, and then it just seemed like a miracle. I know it'll all be worth it."

I nodded. Soon enough, I'd know exactly what Tori was talking about.

"What's the kicking feel like?" I asked. "Does it hurt?"

"Not so much. It can be uncomfortable though," she said. "At first it's almost like butterfly wings in there, and you're not even sure what it is. Then they get stronger and more frequent, and you'll get a jab in the ribs or the bladder or all of a sudden there's an elbow pressed up against you from the inside, and you can even see a bulge. Sometimes Stefan says it looks like I'm carrying an alien in there, but I think of her as my little angel."

"Wow," I said. "I can't imagine."

"Yeah, it's pretty incredible. Stefan and I can't wait to meet her. He's really anxious, but I know he's going to be a great father."

She smiled dreamily, rubbing circles over her belly, and my eyes began to tear up again as I realized that I'd never know that kind of happiness, of expecting a baby with a man who loved me and wanted to share a life with me, who would never hurt me.

Because if Claudia's bombshell had made one thing clear, it was that Ford had never loved me. Our relationship —not just the fake one, but our friendship as well—had been an act all along. A big fat lie. One thing was certain, though —I couldn't fake my way through the next nine months. I needed a real, solid plan.

There was no way I could finish my gelato, so I brought the half-empty pint into the kitchen and tucked it back into the freezer. When I returned to the sofa, Tori was watching TV, still absently stroking her bump.

"Tori," I asked. "Would you ever do it alone? Have a kid, I mean."

Her eyes went wide. "Oh God, I hope I'd never have to. Don't jinx your brother."

"That's not what I meant," I said. "Although if anything happened to Stefan, God forbid, you'd still have all of us. I meant, like—if this had happened in high school or something."

"Oh, I don't know," she finally said. "I mean, I was pretty sheltered back then. I wouldn't have known what to do with a penis if it bit me. Why do you ask?"

Suddenly, she narrowed her eyes and turned her full attention to me.

"You were a virgin?" I blurted out instead, desperately needing to redirect the conversation. "Until when? Weren't you just out of high school when you married Stefan?"

She went red. "Yeah. I met him on my eighteenth birthday. I was...not experienced."

"A virgin bride! Boy did my brother luck out on you, with nobody else to compare him to," I joked. "He must have had his work cut out for him."

Generally I didn't like to talk or even *think* about my brothers' sex lives, but I was doing everything I could to distract my sister-in-law. Luckily, with Tori blushing and sputtering on the other end of the couch, I could tell the subject was officially changed. Which was probably good, because she would have guessed the truth before too long. There was only one real reason why anyone would ask a happily married pregnant woman about single motherhood.

And the last thing I needed was for someone to figure out what I was hiding.

EMZEE

CHAPTER 4

All night, I tossed and turned. Even though Stefan and Tori's guest bedroom was perfectly made up and the bed itself was incredibly comfortable, every time I drifted off to sleep, I'd have bad dreams. Dreams that had me waking in a sweat, heart pounding, adrenaline rushing.

Some of them took me back to high school, where I was forced to relive the torture I'd experienced at the hands of my classmates. In one, I was running down the halls of Wayland-Blaine in my uniform, chased by taunts and cruel laughter, every surface covered with the word WHORE. When I looked down at myself, I found that my arms were covered in slurs too, and no matter what I did, I couldn't scrub them off. Then, just when I thought I couldn't take it anymore, I saw Ford at the end of the hall. Relieved, I ran toward him, knowing he'd save me. But when I grabbed his shoulder and spun him around, his face turned into a demon's.

I definitely didn't need a dream dictionary to tell me what that was all about.

My other dreams were equally stressful and unsubtle.

I'd be alone carrying a bundle that kept getting heavier and heavier, with no one around to help me—but when I pulled back the swaddling, it wasn't a baby in my arms, but a rock.

Worst of all was the dream I had where Ford was holding me, telling me he loved me. It was so real that when I woke up, I started to cry. Because it wasn't real. What I'd had with Ford had never been real. My fairy tale was a lie. That was the nightmare I'd never wake from.

Giving up on sleep around dawn, and totally exhausted, I took a quick shower and slipped back into the pjs Tori had loaned me. Then I padded down the hall like a zombie, focused on getting some coffee in me. It was just before seven, but the unmistakable scent of piping hot java had reached my nose already. Maybe Tori hadn't slept at all.

But when I got to the kitchen, it was Stefan who I blinked at through my bleary eyes. He was leaning against the counter with a steaming mug in his hand, just staring off into space. If anything, he looked like he'd had an even more sleepless night than me.

"Hey," I said, my voice coming out soft and scratchy.

Without a word, he took down a clean mug, filled it with coffee, and handed it to me.

"Sugar? Half and half?"

I smirked. "Come on, bro. You know I take it black. Like my soul."

"Just trying to be a good host."

I walked over to the table and sank into the chair closest to the window, trying to soak up the first rays of morning sunlight. It wasn't until I'd taken the fourth or fifth sip of my coffee that my vision fully cleared.

"You look as exhausted as I feel," I told Stefan. "Tori sleeping in?"

"You could say that." He sighed. "She hasn't been sleeping well the past few weeks. She usually sleeps on her stomach, but that's kind of impossible right now. I think she was up until four just trying to find a comfortable position. I'll be glad when the baby's here."

"We all will. You guys pick out any names yet?"

"We have a short list, but nothing definite. Tori wants to actually see her and hold her in her arms before we make any final decisions."

"That makes sense."

"Pff. I told her the face on the sonogram picture looked like a solid Brunhilda to me, but she wasn't having it."

"You're not naming my niece Brunhilda," I said with a laugh.

"How about Gertrude? I think Trudy is going to be trending again any day now."

Just then, Munchkin trotted into the kitchen, head up, stub of a tail wagging.

"Looks like Munch is the only one who got his eight hours in," I said, kneeling to give him a good ear scratch.

"I never thought I'd be so jealous of a dog," Stefan said.

When I looked back at my brother, he had the broody face on again.

"What's up?" I asked. "Really. It's not just the baby stuff, I can tell."

He let out a sigh and lowered his voice. "I heard from the Bratva."

My stomach dropped. "Again? What do they want?"

"Another payment. I have a little time to figure something out, but I already siphoned funds from our business loan and I can't do that again."

30

"Dad really fucked us," I blurted.

I hated seeing my brother this way. He was about to become a father for the first time, and it should have been one of the best moments of his life, but instead he was tied up in knots over the Russian's mob's threats to blackmail us.

Stefan just shook his head. "I shouldn't even be talking about this. I just...I don't know what we're going to do. What *I'm* going to do."

But I did.

I had a plan, and it all crystalized for me right there at Stefan's kitchen table. The Malones would take care of the Bratva. They had the money and they knew all about what was happening—they knew what the mob wanted from my family and they were willing to pay it in full in order to get me away from their son once and for all. I'd already said yes.

Despite trying to be pragmatic, though, I couldn't help the heartache I felt when I thought about losing Ford. But it was complicated by my new feelings of utter betrayal over what he had done back in high school, and how he had lied about it for the duration of our friendship.

So. The Malones had promised to make all my family's problems disappear as soon as I divorced Ford. All I had to do was make it happen.

He and I had initially agreed that our marriage would last a year, but that timeline was impossible now. With the Bratva breathing down my brother's neck, I would have to file for divorce sooner rather than later. And maybe it was better this way. I had always known that the longer Ford and I stayed together, the harder it would be to protect my heart from getting destroyed when it all ended. But after Claudia's big reveal last night, I wasn't sure I could bounce back from the hurt Ford had caused. Perhaps the pressure

Stefan was getting from the mob was a blessing in disguise. The extra push I needed to cut ties with Ford as soon as possible.

"I have a feeling things will be okay," I said softly. "Call it female intuition."

"I hope you're right," Stefan said, but he still sounded gloomy.

Under the table, I put a hand over my belly. The little life inside me was yet another good reason to call off my marriage. If we split before I started showing, no one would ever have to know the truth about the baby's father. I could simply pretend the new addition to my family involved a sperm donor, or a one-night stand. Or that I'd had a torrid rebound affair after Ford and I broke up. I could make up any lie I wanted to—it wasn't anyone's business.

It was settled, then. Ford's parents would pay out after the divorce went through, per our agreement. All I had to do was keep up my end of the bargain and go through with it. The longer I waited, though, the harder it would be to walk away from my marriage, from the life I'd built with Ford. So maybe the fight we'd gotten in last night was actually a blessing in disguise.

I wouldn't get out of this with my heart fully intact, but I'd have enough of it left. The rest would heal eventually. It would have to. I'd soon have a baby to take care of.

I needed to save my family.

And if that meant lying to Ford and walking away from him, never telling him the truth, then so be it.

"I'm going to take care of it," I told Stefan.

He looked over at me, his expression one of shock.

"No," he said. "This isn't your responsibility."

"It's just as much my responsibility as it is yours," I argued.

"I don't care. I don't want you involved. These people are dangerous."

"Don't worry," I insisted. "I have a plan."

He looked even more startled by that. "What's your plan?"

I shook my head.

"Just let me take care of it," I said.

"Emzee," he said, looking worried. As the oldest Zoric sibling, he'd always shouldered the heaviest burdens, gone out of his way to protect us all—whether it be from our father's verbal abuse or covering for me and Luka to get us out of trouble. Stefan had always come through for us when we needed him most. But now it was time for me to be the hero.

"I need you to trust me," I said. "There's no danger involved, I can promise you that."

I could tell that he wanted to keep arguing, but I wasn't going to back down.

He must have seen the resolve on my face, or maybe it was his exhaustion getting to him. Either way, Stefan finally let out a breath and nodded.

"Okay," he said. "I'll let you give it a try."

CHAPTER 5

I knew Ford wouldn't skip a day of work just because we were fighting, and by the time Munchkin and I Ubered home, my husband was long gone. Perfect.

It was time to put on my battle armor.

Since last night, I'd been avoiding his calls and texts. He wanted to talk, to explain, but I didn't need his explanations. Nothing could excuse the fact that he'd been lying to me for so long. That the high school hell I'd suffered through at the academy was all because of *him*. God, it was humiliating. He'd strung me along for seven years, letting me moon over him and put him on a pedestal as my hero and savior, as if keeping his dirty secret wasn't bad enough already.

Flipping through the dresses in my closet—well, technically my side of Ford's closet—all I kept thinking was that I'd been a fool to trust him. How could I have been so stupid? Ford had been taking advantage of me since day one, up until we were legally married.

And now I was pregnant.

I didn't think things could get any worse.

Holding up a black dress, I looked in the mirror and sighed. Too funereal. I needed something powerful and aggressive, something that would pump up my confidence. An outfit that would remind Mr. and Mrs. Malone, senior, that I was a force to be reckoned with. And also that they had more to gain by paying me off than by letting Ford steamroll over them.

This whole situation was a fucking mess. One thing was certain, though. After this was all over, I didn't want to speak to him. I didn't want to see him. I didn't want anything to do with him or the rest of his family, not ever again.

Unfortunately, before I could wash my hands of the Malones for good, I had to meet with the dreaded in-laws. As long as I kept the news of my pregnancy to myself, I still had leverage. And despite the poor terms we'd left on before the fundraiser (when Ford had burst into their library to "save" me from their threats), I knew they'd welcome me coming back around to their side of things.

Especially considering the fact that the deal I'd made with them included me staying married to Ford for a year. They'd be more than overjoyed to hear that I was interested in exiting the marriage earlier. Way, way earlier.

There was no possibility that they'd question my motives, either. I'd be playing directly into every assumption the elder Malones had ever had about me. To them, I was nothing but nouveau riche trash. And with the Zoric patriarch in jail and our family business in financial jeopardy, why wouldn't I be anything but thrilled to trade in my marriage to Ford for a mountain of cold hard cash? Not that I'd be getting any of it. The Bratva were the only ones who'd be profiting off of this deal.

Ah. *This* was the one. I pulled out a dress I'd never actually worn out in public and held it up to me, nodding as I checked myself out in the full-length mirror. It was a simple sheath dress, but it hugged my body like a glove. The color was a bright lipstick red. Harlot red, I knew Mother Malone would think to herself.

Well, let her. Let her see that I didn't give a damn what she thought of me. This was war.

I slipped the dress off the hanger and threw it over my shoulder, then headed back to the bathroom to finish my makeup.

MY IN-LAWS WERE ALREADY in the library when I was shown into the house by Vivi, the Malones' longtime house-keeper. Of course it had to be the library.

I hated that library.

"Mara," Mrs. Malone said coldly as Vivi ushered me into the room.

"Hello, Mrs. Malone. Mr. Malone. So good to see you again," I lied. I forced myself to smile, as if I didn't have a care in the world.

"You said you wanted to speak to us," Ford's mother said. "Well?"

She was sitting in a burgundy leather wingback chair, a villain's prime choice of seating if I'd ever seen one. Mr. Malone was behind his desk, pointedly ignoring both me and his wife as he hid behind the *Wall Street Journal*. He could be completely charming, I knew from experience— but he was also a total pushover whenever his wife was in the same room. It was like he couldn't stand being around her either, and always chose the path of least resistance. I almost felt sorry for him, but not quite.

Clearing my throat, I lifted my chin and said, "I wanted to discuss our arrangement."

"Did you now?" Mrs. Malone said. I saw the way she was taking in my appearance, and the curl of her lip as she did so. I couldn't help feeling a petty twinge of satisfaction at her obvious disgust. I wanted to strike a pose. To really make her uncomfortable.

"We're all ears," Ford's dad said. "Though to be honest, this hardly comes as a surprise."

Ah. So they assumed I had come over to formally back out of our deal, or at the very least request an extension on the marriage term. After Ford had declared his love for me right in this very library, insisting he wouldn't give me up, and that he'd fight for me, of course it made sense that his parents were expecting me to renege.

Were they in for a shock.

Mr. Malone had actually set his paper down, and was looking at me with an interested expression, which I took as a good sign. It meant I had the floor. The power. I was going to say what I had come to say and they were going to listen.

With a deep breath, I straightened my shoulders and faced the two of them straight on.

"I want out," I said.

"Out of our deal?" Mrs. Malone asked, her voice like acid. "I'm afraid that won't be—"

"No," I interrupted. "Out of the marriage. The sooner the better."

Mrs. Malone's jaw actually dropped. Behind the desk, Mr. Malone's brows lifted.

"*What?*" Mrs. Malone sputtered.

"I don't think we need to keep up this charade for much longer," I said. "You want me and Ford divorced, and I want my family's debt paid." I paused, mustering up the one shred of truth that would give my words the most credence. "The Bratva's been leaning on my brother."

"Ah. I see," Mr. Malone said. He actually sounded sympathetic.

"Nothing is more important to me than my family's security. Including Ford," I added. "I'm sure you understand."

Ford was getting thrown under the bus, but I knew it was necessary. I also knew that the Malones would do whatever it took to get those divorce papers filed as soon as possible.

"And here we thought you were going to try to renegotiate, seeing how you managed to trick our son into *actually* falling for you," Mrs. Malone said.

Her words sliced into me like a knife to my heart. Because I too had thought that Ford was falling for me. After the way he'd defended me to his parents—standing up to them in a way that had surprised me and them—I had believed that our relationship, our marriage, could finally grow into something real. Something based on mutual love and respect. But now I knew that it just wasn't possible. Not after what I'd learned about him. About who Ford really was.

He was just like his parents. Manipulative and self-serving and cruel. The sooner I could purge him from my life, the better off I'd be. The better off my baby would be as well.

"Give me a little credit," I said, surprised at how easily the lies were coming to me. "I intend to honor our deal. Ford's feelings were never part of that."

Lies. Lies. Lies.

I could see that Mrs. Malone didn't fully believe me, but I didn't care. She didn't have to trust my motivations, she just had to trust that we were on the same page when it came to Ford, which, right now, we were.

"Before we move forward with this, though, I need a guarantee that my troubles—my family's troubles—will be over permanently. If I'm going to break my best friend's heart, I need to know the Bratva won't come back. Because if they do, there's no point to any of this."

I looked back and forth between them expectantly. I could tell they hadn't expected me to approach this with such confidence. They had obviously assumed they had the upper hand, and could walk all over me. I felt a rush of adrenaline knowing I was the one in control for once.

The wheels in Mrs. Malone's head were turning. She wanted me out just as much as I wanted myself out. And she didn't want me coming back and causing problems. She wanted me as far away from her precious little Ford as possible.

If she wanted that, she was going to have to pay for it.

"We'll take care of everything," she said after a moment. "You just take care of filling out the paperwork."

She glanced at her husband, and he nodded. "Our lawyers, of course, will go over all of it before you file," he said.

"Perfect," I said.

I didn't care about lawyers, I didn't care about paperwork. I just wanted out.

"And once everything is squared away, that will be it for the two of you," Mrs. Malone said. "For good. No reconciling in the future, or there will be consequences."

I didn't like her tone or her threats, but she didn't have anything to worry about.

"We're done. Forever," I said, even though my chest ached just thinking about it.

I was saying it more for myself than for them, but I could tell I had been convincing. Ford's mom was flashing me a smug, self-satisfied smile that turned my stomach.

"Good," she said. "This will be a clean break."

"It will," I agreed. "As long as you uphold your end of the bargain."

Eschewing the formality of a proper goodbye, I turned my back on them and walked out of the library. As I crossed the threshold, I felt something inside of me break. This was the kind of moment that both my own parents and Ford's must have once had themselves. The moment where money won out over love. Over decency. Over the lives they'd dreamed of having.

The moment they'd left a piece of their soul on the bargaining table.

I could only pray the rest remained intact.

My baby deserved a better parent than the ones Ford and I had gotten.

Vivi tried to talk me into letting the Malones' driver take me home, but I refused. Instead I got an Uber back to Ford's place, and once I was through the door, I fell to my knees and let the tears fall.

It was agony, knowing I was turning my back on Ford forever. Turning my back on a love I had believed was real and genuine. A love I'd tended like a sacred garden for seven years.

But I was also turning my back on the kind of manipulation that my father had used on me and my brothers, the kind that the Malones used on Ford, and were trying to use on me. I was done being a pawn, a plaything. Starting from this day forward, I'd take back my power. I hoped.

Munchkin needing his walk is what finally forced me to pull myself together.

As we circled the block, I told myself I'd done what was necessary. Not just for myself and for my family's business, but for my baby as well. It was better for this little innocent growing inside of me to be raised away from the kind of people the Malones were. My own father was in prison and would never know his grandchild, and I was glad for that. The only people I needed were my brothers and my sisters-in-law. My family. We were enough.

Even knowing that it was all for the best, though, I still hurt. My heart still ached.

And yet there was comfort in knowing that I was going to make sure I was exactly the kind of parent my child deserved. I would do anything—*anything*—to protect this precious spark now growing inside of me.

If that meant I had to break my own heart in the process, then so be it.

FORD

CHAPTER 6

"**M**r. Malone? Mr. Malone? Um...Ford?"

I whipped up my head, realizing I'd been zoning out and that my coffee had long gone cold. Mareena, one of the new paid interns that Malone Real Estate Holdings had hired from Emzee's charity, was standing in the doorway of my office.

"Sorry. How's it going, Mareena?"

She'd been assisting the commercial real estate photographer we had on staff, and the feedback I'd gotten was that we should strongly consider making Mareena a full-time job offer once the term of her internship was up. The photography lessons Emzee offered through See Yourself had set up Mareena perfectly for a new career. If she wanted one, that was.

"Miss Evans wanted to know if you'd finished up with the commercial lease on the Gold Coast property," Mareena said. "She said the client is getting antsy."

"Oh." I looked down at my desk, where the redlined document was still sitting there, unfinished and waiting to be typed up. "Can you let her know I need more time? I'm still going over some of the terms. I'll get it to her this afternoon and then she can fax it over."

"Sure." She hesitated, looking a little concerned.

"Do you need anything? Everybody been treating you okay?" I tried to pay extra close attention to the interns we brought on from See Yourself. Knowing they'd been treated so poorly in the past made me overprotective. I wanted them to feel safe, and confident. Ready to succeed.

Mareena smiled, tucking her dark hair behind her ear. A move that reminded me of my wife. "Everyone's been great. You just look...I don't know, stressed. Distracted. Is it the lease you're working on? Something I can help with?"

This was exactly why Mareena was such an asset to MREH. No matter what needed doing, she was always eager to jump in and assist. That kind of attitude was what made our team so strong. It hadn't always been that way, but with my father mostly-retired, I'd taken the helm more frequently. And when I hired someone new, I didn't look for the pedigree of an Ivy League education or years of experience in real estate. I looked for candidates with keen minds, a willingness to learn, and the ability to stay on top of things even on our most chaotic days.

"I've got this," I said, forcing a smile. "I just have a lot on my plate at the moment. Nothing I can't handle, though. I'll give a shout if I need a hand."

"Okay. Well, you know where to find me."

"Thanks, Mareena."

The second she turned around, my smile dropped. I wasn't just stressed, I was utterly wrecked. All I could think about was Emzee.

It had been over a week since I'd last seen my wife, after See Yourself's fundraiser. She wouldn't answer my calls or texts, wouldn't come to the door when I stopped by Stefan's to try to see her. Hell, I missed Munchkin too. Our little family had been torn apart, and I knew it was all my fault. I should have come clean to Emzee years ago. Now I was paying for it.

I'd hardly slept in days. My productivity at work had gone to shit. And if Mareena was noticing it, everyone else had to be, too. Especially with Miss Evans—my sweet, nearly-retired executive assistant—now keeping tabs on my to-do list. Her usual job functions were answering my phone, scheduling my calendar, and making sure the kitchen was fully stocked. My zombie-like state must have given her the impression that I needed supervision. And maybe I did.

Midway through going over the lease's arbitration exclusions, I realized I'd lost my train of thought again. I couldn't focus like this. My mind was elsewhere. There was nothing I could do to get Emzee to talk to me and it was driving me crazy. I needed her to forgive me, to give me another chance. To give *us* another chance.

Suddenly, I had an idea. I'd send her a gift.

Minimizing the lease agreement, I opened up a browser window on my computer and started browsing reviews and photos for local florists. Maybe flowers were cliché, but I needed to do something to show Emzee that I was sorry. It seemed like a good place to start. I'd probably have to call around to see if anyone could get black orchids on short notice, but—and then I started second-guessing myself. Maybe flowers weren't the way to go at all. Jewelry might be better. It'd definitely last longer. Em wasn't one for lots of flashy accessories, but she appreciated beautiful things. I'd bet anything that she'd love a vintage piece, or something made by a local artist, if it was minimalist and elegant. Subtle enough to wear every day.

I was browsing the Ivy and Rose website when I heard a commotion outside my office.

"You can't see Mr. Malone without making an appointment," Miss Evans was saying, sounding fretful. "I'm sorry, but he's very busy, and we don't offer walk-ins."

"I need to talk to him," a guy coaxed. "It won't take long. Just give me two minutes."

I got up and leaned out of my office door to see what was going on. I didn't recognize the man, but he wore a nice suit and carried a briefcase, and he certainly didn't look dangerous. What if he was from a messenger service? Could he have been sent by Emzee?

"You can't just go back there," Miss Evans argued. "I'll call security."

Rushing to the main reception desk, I said, "Thank you, Miss Evans. I'll handle it."

"You're Ford Malone?" the guy asked.

"I am," I said. "Did Mara Zoric send you?"

"More or less. She wanted me to give this to you," the man in the suit said, handing over a thick envelope. "You've been served."

"I've—wait, what?"

Adrenaline rushing, I ripped open the envelope.

There were divorce papers inside.

When I looked up, I saw that the man—the process server—had already left.

"Mr. Malone?" Miss Evans was saying. "You look like you've seen a ghost."

Her voice sounded a million miles away. My ears were ringing, my stomach was churning. I stood there, speechless and numb, eyes blurring as I skimmed through the pages. My emotions were growing more and more frantic with each word.

I wanted to tear the whole thing up. Set it on fire. Send it through the shredder and then shred it again. On the final page was a small, neon green arrow sticker that said "Sign here."

Like hell was I signing.

"Cancel my meetings for the rest of the day," I told Miss Evans.

"Of course. But the lease agreement—"

"Mareena can finish typing up the changes," I said, cutting her off. "All the redlines are on the doc. I'll drop it with her on my way out."

What the fuck was happening? Emzee couldn't just dump me and run.

I had to get to Stefan's, and fast.

When I arrived at my brother-in-law's place, I rang the bell, pacing in the hall.

But of course when Stefan opened the door, he wouldn't let me inside. We'd done this dance before, but this time I wasn't going to give up.

"I need to see Emzee," I said. "Please."

"She doesn't want to see you," he told me. "Sorry, man."

He started to close the door, but I stuck my foot in the jamb. "Look, I'm not going anywhere until I talk to her," I told him. "I mean it. I'll stay out here as long as I have to."

"I don't care," he said. "Sleep in the hall if you want. But you're not seeing my sister until she's ready to see you. And if that's never, well, tough shit."

"She's my wife," I said, my voice getting louder.

I wasn't above causing a scene. Stefan and I eyed each other. We were both stubborn men. Strong, too. I didn't know if I could take him in a fight if it came to that, but I'd at least go out swinging.

"Don't make me call building security," Stefan said, taking his phone out. "They're not gonna be as nice as I am."

Behind him, a familiar voice said, "Stefan. Wait."

It was Emzee.

Stefan turned away from me, my wife still hidden behind the door. I still had my foot in the doorway and I knew that I could force my way inside. But I waited. Took a deep breath.

"I'll talk to him," she said.

He frowned. "Are you sure?"

"Yes," I heard Emzee say. "It will be the last time."

I couldn't believe it. It made me sick to hear her say the words, but I didn't argue. A second later she stepped out into the hallway, shutting the door behind her. Obviously I wasn't going to get invited inside. But it hardly mattered. All I cared about was Em.

She looked exhausted. I wanted to scoop her up in my arms and take her home. Draw her a bath, put her to bed, make her the green tea she liked. Take care of her.

For a moment, neither of us spoke. She wouldn't even look at me.

"The last time?" I repeated. "Please, Em. Let's figure things out. I'm not signing this."

I held up the divorce papers, shaking my head. Still bewildered by all of it.

"It's what I want," she said firmly.

"We can't be over because of something that happened almost a decade ago. Can we talk about it?" I asked, trying to keep the anger out of my voice.

"No. What's done is done. Nothing you can say will

change what you did, and you can't take back all the years you lied to me. Do you realize that every important man in my life has lied to me? My father, my brothers, and now you. All of you thought you were protecting me by keeping secrets about the trafficking! Do you have any idea how humiliating that is? Knowing I just walked around oblivious to it all, and meanwhile lives were getting destroyed? You should be ashamed! And I know if it wasn't for Claudia, you would have just kept on lying!"

Breathing hard from her rant, she met my gaze. My stomach clenched with guilt and regret and shame. She was right. Her whole life she'd been lied to by men. I was no exception.

"How can this be it? I fucked up, Em, I admit that, but— I *love you*. I know you love me."

She was looking at the floor again, her expression hard and flat. I'd never seen this side of her before. It wasn't that we hadn't fought before, of course we had, but she'd always forgiven me. I'd always been able to lay on the charm and convince her to do things my way.

"You seriously want to throw away everything we have? Everything we could be? Let me make it up to you. Let me show you that I'm not the person I used to be, that I can—"

"Shut *up*." Her voice was sharp and a little bit nasty. "I'm not doing this with you. Everything you say is a lie. Our entire relationship is a lie."

"But it's not. You're my *wife*."

"The marriage isn't real, Ford!" she said. "This whole thing was just an easy way for you to get out of marrying Claudia because you couldn't stand up to your parents. You never cared about me, you just needed me to play my part. The stupid thing is that even though I knew it was all fake, I actually thought our friendship was real. Now I know better."

"Our friendship was real. *Is* real," I argued. "Jesus. You're my best friend."

"Honestly, Ford? That's really kind of pathetic. I almost feel sorry for you."

Then she laughed, right in my face. It stung. She'd never treated me like this before. Had never been so unmovable, so dismissive.

"It's over," she said. "The sooner you realize it, the easier it will be for both of us."

"Emzee, please. I need you. I fucking love you. Please, don't do this—"

Before I could say more, she turned on her heel and went back inside, slamming the door in my face. Leaving me begging in the hallway, practically on my knees.

Fuck.

Back in my car, head in my hands, I tried to get my breathing under control. The world was spinning out of control, taking my stomach with it. How could this be happening?

I knew I deserved her wrath, knew that I'd royally fucked up, but she wasn't giving me a chance to explain. I'd kept secrets from her, yes, but I'd had good intentions. Because if I had tried to tell her why I'd started those rumors at Wayland-Blaine, why I'd targeted her in the first place, I would have had to admit that it was because my father had been a client of her father's prostitution ring. And the reason I never told her about KZ Modeling's illicit underbelly was because I thought it was better if she didn't know. Safer. Hell, finding out about my own parents' issues is what fucked *me* up so badly in the first place. I didn't want that for her.

But trying to protect Emzee had only made her more vulnerable. And it was me who had ended up hurting her. I'd been the one to do the most damage. I'd gone about things all wrong. I could see that now, in hindsight.

I could also see exactly why she wanted to be done with me.

But I wasn't done with her. Emzee was my world. And that little dog of hers, too.

So I was going to have to start over, then. Figure out a way to win her back. I'd never been one to give up on something—or someone—that really mattered to me, and I wasn't about to start.

I'd fight for the woman I loved, and I'd fucking win. Or else I'd die trying.

EMZEE

CHAPTER 7

I 'd only been in New York for a month, but in some ways it felt like an eternity.

After a few weeks of licking my wounds at my brother's place, I'd finally made a call to Andrew Apellido, Editor-in-Chief of *lookingglass* magazine (and recent recipient of a black eye from my soon-to-be ex-husband). The first thing he'd said on the phone was, "I hope you called to tell me you're ready to be our photography editor, because the position's still got your name on it." I had accepted on the spot.

Convincing my brothers that I was making the right choice for myself took some work, but in the end they were supportive. They wanted what was best for me and my career, and they knew the divorce situation with Ford was destroying me. I even helped them interview and hire a new in-house photographer to take over for me at Danica Rose Management, although Stefan insisted on making it a temp-to-hire position just in case I changed my mind in six months and decided to move back to Chicago.

Meanwhile, I told a half-lie to Emma, my administrative

assistant and program coordinator at See Yourself, explaining that I had some high-priority work projects to take care of over the next few weeks and that I'd need her to cover for me for a bit. I felt bad for skipping town like a thief in the night, but I was too overwhelmed to do anything other than run.

With Stefan's help (he knew a great real estate broker in the city), I arranged a short-term lease on a gorgeous prewar apartment in an artsy area of Brooklyn, just over the Williamsburg Bridge and about a twenty-minute subway ride to Manhattan. The neighborhood was great, and I felt like I blended in with my black combat boots and my leather jacket, but on the inside, I was struggling. It had been quite an adjustment so far. Actually, I wasn't sure I'd adjusted much at all. Chicago was a village compared to the chaotic 24/7 hustle and bustle of New York. Even Munchkin seemed to be having a hard time.

Probably just because everything was new to us. New job, new apartment, new streets and sights and smells. No reminders of Chicago at all...if I didn't count the prenatal vitamins. I'd been keeping fairly busy, but at night, trying to fall asleep, Ford always seemed present. My grief was still so raw that it seemed like there would never be an escape. I hadn't spoken to him since that day he showed up at Stefan's condo with the divorce papers in his hand.

God bless the millennial habit of dog-friendly work-places—it meant I got to keep Munch at my side all day for company, and I never had to feel guilty about the long hours I'd been pulling. My dog spent most of the day curled up under my desk, though sometimes I dropped him off at the doggie spa down the street. There was also a cute bakery a few blocks away that sold these cupcake-shaped dog treats called pupcakes, and every few days I'd walk Munchkin there to get him one.

"Working late again?"

Andrew's voice startled me out of the photo editing zone I'd been in for the last few hours. I looked up at my new boss's handsome face, all kindness and concern, and did my best to return the smile he was giving me.

"Can't help it," I said. "The early days are the ones that set the tone. I'm not turning in anything less than perfection."

I knew I wasn't expected to put in the kind of hours I had been clocking, but I desperately needed the distraction. Not only that, but I wanted to make the best possible impression on my coworkers and the *lookingglass* subscribers.

"I'd expect nothing less from the great Emzee Zoric," he said. "You've been a godsend to the magazine. Though I'm sure your brothers aren't happy with me for poaching you."

"Nah, they were okay with it. A little shocked, maybe, but they've been supportive. They knew I was ready for a challenge."

He nodded. "Well, don't push yourself too hard. And let me know when you want to grab a drink after work. All work and no play, right?"

I raised a brow. The last time we'd gotten drinks, the night had ended with Andrew and Ford in fisticuffs. Or I guess, more accurately, the two of them at an Urgent Care.

Andrew must have known exactly what I was thinking. "Completely platonic drinks, colleague to colleague. In fact, we can invite the whole office. And your husband, if he's ready to forgive me my trespasses. My treat."

Ah. There it was. I'd been waiting for him to mention Ford. So far, Andrew had been such an incredible boss—

and friend—to me. Not only had he given me a job, my dream job, really, but he'd been kind enough not to ask too many questions about why I'd called out of the blue to accept his job offer. Ford's name hadn't even come up until now...though I knew he had to be extremely curious about why I'd suddenly changed my mind about moving to New York, and what that move meant for my marriage.

"Actually, he's still in Chicago," I said. Better to get the truth out of the way than make up some elaborate lie that I wouldn't be able to maintain. "We're sort of...separated."

"Oh wow. I'm so sorry," Andrew said sincerely. "I'd wondered."

I shook my head. "It's fine. I mean, I'll be fine. I'd rather not talk about it."

"Yeah. Of course. Totally respect that." He stepped back with his hands up, as if to prove that he was happy to literally and figuratively give me space. Honestly, I appreciated it. "Well, let me know if you need anything. I'll leave you to it."

"Thanks, Andrew. Have a good night."

He headed out, turning off most of the office lights on his way, and then I was alone. Leaning back in my chair, I stretched, hoping I could squeeze out just a few more photo edits before I went home.

But first I reached down and gave Munchkin a treat and a scratch behind his ears. He wagged his stubby tail happily.

"That's my good boy," I told him, but my voice cracked and my eyes started to sting. Sometimes the weight of everything snuck up on me like that, out of nowhere. The loss heavy in my chest. The memories of my last moments with Ford replaying in my head on repeat.

I hadn't expected him to sign the divorce papers without a fight, but it had been agony to face him in that hallway and tell him that we were over. I knew it was the right thing to do—knew that he couldn't repair what he had broken—but it still hurt. Maybe it always would. I wasn't sure I'd ever truly get over him.

Because it felt like so many bereavements at once. I'd lost not just my husband and my happily ever after, but also the friendship I'd always depended on and the entire basis of it. People talked about the rug being yanked out from under you, but in my case, it turned out the entire floor had been rotten all along. The rug was just another pretty lie.

I saved the image I'd been working on and closed out of my editing program. Then, out of habit, I checked my email for a message that I was starting to think would never come.

The one from my lawyer that would confirm that Ford had signed the divorce papers.

But per usual, there was nothing from the firm. No matter how many hundreds of times I refreshed my inbox, I never got the email I was waiting for.

Instead, I had yet another message from Mrs. Malone. Berating me for the fact that her son still refused to sign and file the paperwork that would end our union. Reminding me that they wouldn't settle my family's debt until the divorce was finalized. As if it was my fault.

I sent back a terse reply, telling Ford's mother the same things I always did. That I'd held up my end of the bargain, and I wanted him to sign those papers just as much as she did, but there wasn't anything I could do. That I was just as anxious as they were for our agreement to go through, and that I looked forward to the matter being resolved as soon as possible.

Not that she cared that the hold-up wasn't actually my fault. The Malones weren't the kind of people who took responsibility for anything, so why would they even consider sitting their son down and having a chat? Though, truth be told, it probably wouldn't do anything to change Ford's mind. He was too stubborn. And it was doubtful they had any influence over him.

It was time to take matters into my own hands.

Though the thought of calling Ford to beg him to sign the papers made me sick—or maybe that was nausea from my pregnancy. I was starting to wonder when the supposed pregnancy glow would kick in, because so far, I'd mostly just felt like crap.

I got myself a glass of water from the office kitchen and then pulled Munchkin into my lap, phone in my hand. This was it. I'd been putting off this call long enough.

Assuming Ford answered, I'd be as direct as possible. I'd tell him that I needed him to sign off on the divorce immediately, that things were completely over between us, that he couldn't undo the hurt he had caused and the distrust I had for him. There was no going back.

Even if there was a way for him to make amends, I couldn't allow it. I needed this divorce to go through so I could save my family. The only people in my life who hadn't betrayed me. I wanted to do this for them—for Stefan and Tori, for Luka and Brooklyn, for my soon-to-be nieces and nephews. I wanted their lives to be free of the constant threat from the Russian mob. I wanted all of us to be free. I just needed Ford to cooperate.

Steeling myself, I pressed the call button.

It only rang once before he picked up. I didn't even wait for him to speak before I started talking. This was already painful enough, and the sound of his voice might just break my heart into too many tiny pieces to cope with.

"Listen, Ford, I need you to sign the papers. It's time," I said in a rush, struggling to keep my voice cool and detached. "I know this is sooner than we'd planned, but it was always going to end like this. In divorce. That was always the deal. So just...let it end. You can't fix what you've broken, and I don't want you to try. The only thing I want is for you to let me go. I'm not going to change my mind. Please stop making this harder than it already is."

I held my breath, desperate to hear him say that he would do what I'd asked.

"I have no intention of making this easy," he said.

I tightened my grip on Munchkin, my knees going weak to hear his voice. It was so close, so clear, it almost sounded like he was in the same room.

That's when I heard a sound behind me.

Turning slowly in my chair, I found Ford standing on the other side of the office, phone to his ear. He was here.

He'd come to New York.

FORD

CHAPTER 8

I could tell Emzee was shocked to see me standing there. She was still sitting in her chair, mouth slightly open. Meanwhile, Munchkin had jumped off her lap and raced over to me. He was at my feet, looking up expectantly. At least someone was glad I was there.

"Hi," I said to my wife. God, she was beautiful. Seeing her face was like reaching the surface after half drowning in the ocean, and getting that first oxygen-laced lungful of fresh air. I crouched down to pet our dog, trying to hide my emotion. "Hey, pup. You missed me? Yeah?"

My one-sided conversation with the dog seemed to snap Emzee back to reality. She stood up, arms crossed, narrowing her eyes at me.

"You shouldn't have shown up here like this," she said.

"Em—" I got to my feet, but she put a hand out, stopping me from coming any closer.

"If you don't go, I'll have you escorted out of the building by security," she threatened.

"I need to talk to you."

She was shaking her head at me, looking as pissed as I'd

ever seen her. "This is completely unprofessional. God, I can't believe you're bringing this drama to my new job."

"*Me* bring the drama?" Was she serious? I wasn't the one who'd picked up and moved to another city to start a new job without so much as mentioning it to my spouse. If anyone had acted dramatically, it had been her—but I wasn't going to bring that up. I was trying to win her back, not pick a fight.

"We're not doing this, Ford. I'm calling the front desk."

She leaned over her desk and grabbed the receiver of an office landline phone, already pushing a button on the console.

"Okay, okay. I'll leave," I said, backing up. "For now."

Emzee kept the phone in her hand, watching me. "Go. I'm waiting."

Her voice was as cold as I remembered it being the last time I'd seen her. Like I meant less than nothing to her. Which couldn't be true—I just didn't believe it. Not after everything we'd been through over the last seven years. Though when I found out she'd uprooted her entire life to move to New York, it had been a sobering moment. Still, I had hope.

Without another word, I turned and left.

Not that I was giving up. Far from it. Instead, I got a coffee from a little industrial style café a few doors down. Then I sat myself on a bench outside her building, which is where I was waiting when she finally walked out of the lobby a little while later. Munchkin was straining at his leash trying to get to me, and Emzee let out a frustrated sigh as the two of them came over.

"This is what's known as stalking," she said. "I don't want you showing up here again, or at my apartment, or anywhere near me. I'll get a restraining order if I have to."

I shrugged. "I'm not signing those papers until we at least have a discussion. That's all I'm asking. You owe me that much at least." I searched her eyes, looking for a hint of softness, but didn't find any.

"Honestly, I don't owe you anything, but fine. The café?" she asked, pointing toward the place where I'd just gotten my coffee.

She'd finally given in. She must have really wanted those papers signed, our marriage over and done with as soon as possible.

"Let's go to my place," I suggested. "It's in Brooklyn. I'll get a car."

Her brows shot up. "You have a place here?"

"Yup." I expertly hailed us a cab, promising the driver I'd pay extra if Munchkin made any kind of mess in the back seat. As I directed the driver to go east over the bridge, I watched Emzee's expression from the corner of my eye. She was looking more and more on edge the closer we got to my address in Williamsburg.

When the cab pulled to the curb to drop us off, she turned to me with a look of shock.

"This is *my* building," she said.

"It's my building, too," I told her as we got out.

"You got an apartment in my building?"

I nodded. "I'm in the process of buying the whole building, actually. By the way, you don't have to pay rent anymore."

She snapped her mouth closed and stalked into the lobby, refusing to acknowledge me even as we got in the elevator and I pushed the button for the top floor.

It wasn't until we were inside, Munchkin off his leash and the door closed and locked, that she dropped her bags and laid into me, her expression livid.

"How *dare* you invade my space like this!" she raged. "How dare you chase me all the way here, when I couldn't have made it clearer that I want this to be over? Please, just sign the divorce papers and leave me alone."

Munchkin had been sniffing around the place, but at the sound of Emzee's outburst, he had run over to cower behind my legs. I picked him up, patting his back as he panted anxiously.

That only seemed to make Emzee more furious.

"Even my dog is betraying me!" she yelled.

"He knows that I'm sorry," I said.

She ignored me, reaching for Munchkin. I let her take him, watching her turn away and walk toward the windows in the living room as she clutched him to her chest.

"Do you have any idea," she said, her back to me, "how hard you're making it for me to get over you?"

My heart nearly stopped. I turned her words over in my mind a few times, just to make sure I understood what she was saying. Then I crossed the room to stand closer to her.

"Then don't get over me," I pleaded, staying far enough away to not crowd her. The last thing I wanted was to invade her space, or do anything that would have her throwing all her defenses up again. This was my opening, as tiny as it was, and I was taking it.

She'd just admitted that she still had feelings for me.

"Why are you fighting me so hard, Em?"

Finally she set the dog down and turned to look at me, her eyes stormy and edged with tears. I stepped closer, knowing that this was my moment. That if I could just kiss her, I could get her to remember what we had together.

I lowered my head, and she lifted hers. Our gazes locked. Time stopped. The chemistry between us was unmistakable, the familiar, magnetic pull almost palpable.

But when I'd gotten close enough to feel her breath on my lips, she gasped and pushed me away. Like she'd suddenly come to her senses and realized what was about to happen. The spell was broken.

"I'm leaving," she said, scooping up Munchkin.

She grabbed the bags she'd left at the door and walked out of my apartment. I ran after her, watching her stride down the hall toward the elevator. The doors slid open, and just as she was about to step in, I called out to her.

"I'm still not signing the papers, Em," I said.

EMZEE

CHAPTER 9

S neaking myself and Munchkin in and out of my apartment building had become an elaborate operation, the likes of which would have probably impressed the KGB.

Once we even spent the night at the *lookingglass* offices, but unfortunately all the couches there were designed for appearance, not comfort. Munchkin slept just fine in the dog bed that I kept under my desk, but I wasn't so fortunate. Waking up at dawn with an aching back and a sore neck to hurriedly change and brush my teeth in the bathroom down the hall had made me feel like some sort of criminal. It wasn't something I'd be repeating again.

Plus, I liked my apartment. I didn't want to have to sleep at work. I wanted to be in my own home. But everywhere I turned, there Ford was. Holding the elevator for me, leaving flowers and dog treats on the mat outside my door, doing work on his laptop in the building's lobby while overseeing some much-needed repairs, like the cracks in the marble floor tiles—which I had to admit now looked great.

He just kept on schmoozing me, using all of the

patience and romance I'd spent years yearning for. What an irony; now that I was finally getting Ford's full attention, I needed it to stop. To make matters even worse, the pregnancy was wreaking havoc with my hormones. Which meant I was super horny all the time. Which was obnoxious and unhelpful.

I was still completely taken aback by the whole situation. What the hell was he trying to pull? Why wouldn't he just accept that we were over, sign the damn papers, and leave me alone?

But I knew why. It was because Ford Malone had never walked away from something he wanted. And he wanted me.

I had to stay strong. I told myself he didn't even really want me, he just didn't want to *lose* me. He didn't want to lose, period. Even if we did get back together, there was no guarantee he wouldn't get bored after a while and decide to go through with the divorce as planned. At which point I'd be in the same boat I was in now, except that I would have totally fucked my opportunity to have the senior Malones pay off the Bratva. Not a gamble I was willing to take.

Having him in the same building was risky enough. Five minutes alone with him and I'd almost lost control of myself, almost threw myself at him with no regard for the consequences. The only thing I could do to make sure I kept up my end of the deal with the Malones was to stay as far away from Ford as possible. It had been so hard to resist him, and I wasn't sure that I'd be able to a second time if it happened again.

Because despite everything, I still wanted him. He was who I thought of at night, in the shower, when I got lost in a daydream at work. Ford Malone. Years of pining for him had left a permanent scar on my heart, a default desire for him that I just couldn't shake. It was maddening.

Which meant that I had to avoid him at all costs.

Unfortunately, the fact that he now owned and lived in my building made that extremely difficult. He would offer to walk Munchkin, or even take him for the entire day so I didn't have to keep taking him to work. I refused, of course, but he just kept asking. There were times I'd answer a knock on my door after a late night at work to find that Ford had ordered takeout for me, or arranged to have groceries delivered. It was all very sweet, and also very infuriating.

I had thought, at least, that work would be my refuge—and it was, at first. Mainly because I had alerted all the security guards to his presence and made it clear that he wasn't to be allowed into the building under any circumstances, and to call the police if he walked in.

So Ford stayed away from the office. I was safe at last.

Until he found a way around my imposed ban.

It didn't take long for him to figure out a loophole, and it involved an endless stream of packages to my desk. Exotic floral arrangements, pastel-colored macarons from Ladurée, gourmet catered lunches and various ridiculous gift baskets for the whole office. He even arranged for a barbershop quartet to show up one day and serenade us. I became not just a running office joke, but a target of my coworkers' envy.

But as the beneficiaries of Ford's deliveries, they all soon became frequent visitors to my desk. I gave away everything he sent, and people were thrilled to take cashmere sweaters and Diptyque candles and MarieBelle chocolates home with them. They were sympathetic to my plight, initially. They'd cluck understandingly when another unwelcome package arrived and share in my frustration when I told them I just wanted to be left alone. They seemed to understand how annoying and disruptive Ford's constant attempts to get my attention were.

But since they all got to freely indulge in the constant barrage of luxurious gifts while I was self-righteously and steadfastly refusing them, it wasn't long before he'd managed to build up a pretty supportive chorus around the water cooler. A few of my colleagues even asked if I was perhaps overreacting to whatever Ford had done.

"Clearly he's really sorry," Natasha from the IT desk had told me one day. "A man working so hard for forgiveness should be heard out, at least?"

It was total bullshit. They were *my* coworkers, and Ford had managed to win all of them over to his side, all without setting foot in the office. It was typical. He'd never met a woman he couldn't charm, and now I was surrounded by colleagues who had joined forces to support his cause: getting me to forgive him.

I knew if I told them what had really happened, about the lies Ford had told and the years of trauma he had caused me, they might think twice about taking his side. But all I'd shared was that I was trying to divorce him. I'd even used the standard term—taken directly from my divorce papers —*irreconcilable differences*. I had no desire to explain the whole story in all its gory details, the layers of obfuscation. It was too horrible and too personal.

When they asked, I just told them that all his gifts were a drop in the bucket compared to what he had done. I knew they thought I was being a drama queen, but I didn't care. They weren't my friends. Besides my family, I'd never actually had any of those, it turned out.

Thank God for Tori and Brooklyn. Without their texts and calls to keep my spirits up, I would have been totally on my own. Even still, every day it got harder and harder to stay strong. To resist the pull of Ford Malone.

Today had been especially hard.

I'd arrived at the office to find my desk covered with my favorite flowers—orchids. In every color imaginable, from pale pink to deep purple-black. They were so beautiful that my pregnancy hormones almost made me cry at the sight of them. They were all in planters, so I gave away as many as I could, but I kept a few of them for my desk. It was the only thing Ford had sent so far that I'd decided to keep, and I was conflicted about it, but I decided a few plants couldn't really hurt. He would never have to know that I'd kept them.

But the blooms didn't escape the notice of some of the editors on staff. A few of which had been the most vocal about their opinions that I should maybe reconsider my divorce. Two of them stopped by my desk after lunch to ooh and ahh.

"So thoughtful," one of them said, practically swooning.

"What I wouldn't do for *my* partner to shower me with flowers," the other one sighed.

"It's like your own private botanical garden," the first added. "Very romantic."

I had just smiled and pretended to be super focused on my computer screen, but their words had sunk in deep.

By the time I headed out to supervise a photoshoot for the magazine, I couldn't stop thinking about everything Ford had done to show me that he was sorry, that he cared, that he wanted me. I hated that he'd gotten so involved in my new life without permission, but I couldn't deny that he'd done a lot to make my adjustment to New York City easier. Like leaving a map of all the local dog parks in my mailbox, having my favorite wine delivered, and finding a really good Chicago-style pizza place that he knew would remind me of home.

Hooking back up with him was absolutely not an option, but damn, I was feeling susceptible lately.

Arriving at the address in Chelsea, I was already physically and emotionally exhausted. But I knew I had to pull myself together and make the magic happen. Andrew had given me full creative control, which was amazing, but it also meant that I had a lot more responsibility than I'd ever had at Danica Rose. As the photography editor-in-chief, I wasn't just shooting my own photos, I was overseeing other photographers and shoots as well.

It wasn't until I was already walking onto the set that I realized the shoot I'd be overseeing was all nude. I'd been so distracted by everything happening in my personal life that I hadn't prepared the way I usually did, hoping that I could just show up and wing it. A mistake I would never let myself make again.

"Emzee, you're here! Fantastic!" said Rian, an up-and-coming freelancer we'd just hired for the first time. I'd seen her photos in a gallery one day while walking Munchkin and had immediately reached out to see if she'd be interested in shooting a series for *lookingglass*. Needless to say, she was already a fan of mine for hooking her up with the gig.

"Hey!" I said, trying not to look like a deer in headlights. "This all looks great. You want to show me your shot list before you get started?"

Rian practically jumped up and down. "Yes! This is so exciting!"

I'd shot plenty of nudes, and I'd obviously been surrounded by naked models before, but never while pregnant—and in my fragile state, I found myself turned on to no end.

The shoot was agonizingly long, and I spent most of it trying to maintain my composure as I watched a pair of sultry, smudgy-eyelinered models with amazing chemistry pose together in various sensual positions, their bodies wrapped around each other like vines. Rian was really into hands and the angles and curves of the body, so there was a lot of grabbing and bending and giggling involved. An assistant was on standby with a spray bottle to add water droplets to bare skin, and the hair stylist made sure no one's sexy bedhead fell flat. Meanwhile the models were obviously having a great time, probably because Rian's energy was so contagious.

By the time we wrapped, I was so hot and bothered that I could barely focus. All I wanted to do was go home and get my vibrator out and take care of the persistent throb of desire that was coursing through my veins. The subway ride back to Brooklyn had never taken so long.

But when I finally stepped off the elevator on my floor, I could already see Ford at the end of the hall, leaning on the wall beside my apartment door. He looked adorably rumpled in his suit, and had probably been waiting a long time—I was home extra late, even for me.

Munchkin pulled at the leash, panting with happiness, and I let him run to Ford.

Seeing him crouch down to pet my dog, something inside me cracked.

I couldn't resist anymore.

FORD

CHAPTER 10

I didn't know what I'd done to win Emzee over, but at the moment I didn't really care—because she was all over me and that was the only thing that mattered.

After pulling me into her apartment, she'd put Munchkin in the bedroom, pushed me onto the couch, and started ripping off my clothes. I'd rarely seen her so aggressive before, but as long as she was letting me in, I was going to take advantage of the opportunity. Make her mine again.

We were groping each other on the couch, tongues tangled, half dressed and frantic. The feel of her body against mine was everything. I had missed stroking my hands over her curves, squeezing the globes of that perfect ass, kissing the soft skin of her neck, her shoulders, her breasts. The glide of my tongue against her tightening nipples, her breathless moans in my ear.

We didn't even make it to the bedroom before her hands were sliding down between us, her hot grip finding my cock and squeezing me through my briefs. I was rock hard and ready, but there was something else I'd missed so badly I couldn't wait another second for it—so I pushed her into a seated position against the cushions and slid onto the floor to kneel between her legs.

I hooked my fingers into the waistband of her underwear and started teasing them down slowly, never breaking eye contact with her. My plan was to remind her exactly what she'd been living without, starting from the bottom and making my way up. I'd take my time about it, too. Make her ache for it. For me.

Once I had her fully naked in front of me, I slid my hands up her thighs, pushing her legs wide apart. I could see her pussy glistening, pink and wet. Fuck. She was so ready for me. My cock was so hard it hurt, and I shifted a little, adjusting myself in my briefs before burying my face in that sweet, sweet cunt. Emzee instantly let out a moan, grinding against my tongue.

God, yes.

She was even wetter than I expected, tasting as sweet as a peach, practically gushing in my mouth like ripe fruit. I dragged my tongue up her slit and then around her clit as she gasped for air above me, her hips jerking as I fucked her with my mouth. Sucking, lapping, thrusting into her with my tongue. Her hands had gone to her breasts, squeezing them together, and she fingered her nipples as she rode my mouth. It was a beautiful sight. I couldn't get enough.

I dipped my tongue deeper inside her, wanting to feel her come against my mouth. I needed her to remember how good it was when we were together. How good I could be to her.

She threw her head back, eyes closed as I sucked on her clit again. Soft and steady, just the way she liked it. Her hands slid down into my hair, pulling me hard against her, and I loved it. I tensed my tongue and slid it back and forth inside her, giving her a taste of what she'd experience with my cock until she was moaning louder, her cries shorter and faster as her hips began to buck harder beneath me. I knew she was getting close. I slipped two fingers inside her, moving my mouth up to capture her clit, sucking with the firm, gentle pressure she loved.

"I'm coming," she warned, fingers tightening in my hair, her thighs squeezing the sides of my head. "Ford...I'm going to come."

And then she did, crying out, body writhing against the couch cushions.

I licked her through the shudders of her orgasm, reveling in the taste of her. When her breath began to slow and her body began to relax, I started anew, thrusting my tongue inside of her again first and then stretching her wide with my fingers. Two and then three, in a twisting motion, and then I curled them inside her to rub the pad of her G-spot.

She went wild when I did, her hands gripping the couch cushions, holding on to them for dear life as she cursed softly.

"Good girl. Just relax. Just like that," I coaxed, determined to make her come again before I even took my cock out, even though it was screaming for my attention.

The sounds she was making, those low, breathy moans, those husky cries alternating between my name and a stream of swear words, were making me even harder, which I had thought was damn near impossible. I wanted her so bad I could barely see straight, focusing all of my attention on her pleasure.

Slipping my free hand under her ass, I angled her hips so I had better access, my lapping tongue and stroking fingers bringing her closer and closer to release.

"Come for me, Emzee," I whispered, lifting my head. "Come on, baby."

Finally, I felt her go over the edge, losing control—her inner muscles clenching around my fingers as she wailed so loudly I was pretty sure all the neighbors could hear it. Probably the entire block could hear it.

This time, I didn't wait for her to stop shuddering. I stood up and gazed down at her, my cock in my hand, dripping with precum. I moved her onto her back and then lowered myself onto the couch between her thighs, making a space for myself there.

"You want this cock, or have you had enough?" I asked her, knowing she'd never say no.

Her eyes were glassy with pleasure but I could see the hunger there. She wanted more. She wanted all of me.

"I want it," she said. "I want you to fuck me."

I groaned at the sound of those words, words I hadn't heard in far too long, and I pushed her knees up against her chest and slid my cock inside her.

We both moaned as I seated myself as deep as possible. It had been so long and yet, it felt like no time had passed at all. Even though I'd already given her two orgasms, she was still so tight that my eyes practically rolled back in my head.

"Fuck," I panted, going still, using all my willpower not to come right then and there. She was so wet, so sweet, so tight.

"Mmm, that feels good," she murmured. I could feel her pussy tightening around me, pulsing softly. "So fucking good."

"You want this cock?" I asked again as I began to fuck her slowly. "Tell me you want this cock. Say it."

It sounded like she was praying as she said, "I want it. I

want it. Fuck, I want it. I want that big, hard cock. Give it to me."

Even though my entire body was begging me to take her fast and hard, I didn't. My rhythm was slow and steady, with both of us staring into each other's eyes the entire time. This wasn't just fucking, it wasn't just sex. This was making love. I was making love to her. Using my body to show her exactly what she meant to me.

I could tell that she felt it, her hands squeezing my biceps as she looked up at me, searching for something unknowable. Unable to stand it, I leaned down and kissed her, losing myself in the moment. I wanted this to last forever. Wanted to drink her up.

Parting her knees, I lifted them around my waist so we could be as close as possible as I thrusted deeper and deeper. Sweat began to gather at my temples as my own control began to fray. I was close, but there was no fucking way I was going to come before she did.

Emzee whimpered as I dipped my head down to her tits and used my teeth and tongue to tease the hard peaks of her nipples. They seemed even more sensitive than I remembered, and I had barely turned my attention to her second breast when she started gasping beneath me, her nails digging into my arms, her pussy contracting in tight bursts around my cock as she came for the third time.

I fucked her all the way through it, and then, as she sagged back into the couch, all tension released from her body, I let myself go, spurting hard and deep inside her. My entire body was tingling, the climax radiating through my body from my head to my toes.

"Em," I groaned, still coming. It took a few minutes for my orgasm to taper away, and I rested my head on her chest as I slowly caught my breath. Sex between us had always been amazing, but this felt different. Like coming home. I was sure she'd felt it, too.

I raised my head to kiss her, relieved that we were back on track. That things could go back to the way they'd been before Claudia had ruined everything. It would take a lot of work, yes, and I knew I had a long road ahead of me to fully earn back her trust, but I'd do whatever it took to make things right. But before our lips could meet, Emzee turned her face away.

"You need to go," she said.

My stomach dropped. "What?"

"Get off me."

What the hell?

Confused, I got up slowly, finding my clothes and getting dressed as she continued to look everywhere else but at me.

"Em. I don't want to leave," I told her, buttoning my pants.

"We both got what we wanted," she said. "Now go."

I couldn't believe my ears. "I didn't come here for sex. That's not what I want from you. I want our *relationship*. I love you."

She shook her head. "This was a mistake."

"No, it wasn't. I love you," I repeated. "And I know you love me."

That got her to look at me, although it was more of a glare. "You lied to me," she said.

It was the truth, and it hit me like a knife in the gut.

"Yes. I did lie to you. And it ate me up inside all these years, but I was so scared of losing you that I couldn't make myself tell you the truth," I said, sitting down on the couch next to her. She curled up as far away from me as possible, pulling her knees to her chest.

I went on, "I'm so, so sorry for everything that happened in high school. I was young and angry and completely self-centered. It was never about you. It was about me. I was lashing out. That day, with the lockers. I'd gone home and overheard my parents arguing about my dad's infidelities, and my mom was crying. That's when I found out about your dad and the...the women at KZM. It shattered me. I thought they were going to get a divorce over the whole thing. And when I got back to school, I saw you in the quad, and I just...lost it."

She was listening, I could tell, but she didn't respond. She wouldn't engage. My words weren't getting through. I got down on my knees in front of her, taking her hand.

"I've regretted it ever since. Honestly, I had no idea it would blow up like it did. That's why I had to defend you, finally. I knew I was wrong, and I knew it was all my fault you were catching shit. If I could take it all back, I would. God, I wish I could. Please believe me. I'm sorry, Emzee," I said. "I know I fucked up, but what we have is too good to walk away from."

She shook her head. "I'm sorry," she said. "I'm really sorry. But I can't. We can't."

I didn't understand. *Can't?*

"What do you mean?" I asked. "Is it my parents? Fuck them. Fuck what they think."

A sad smile crossed her face. "It's not your parents, Ford. We were just never meant to be together. This thing with us, it's...over."

How could she say that? How had it even gotten this bad? She was my best friend. I was hers. Or at least, I thought I'd been. In fact, now that I thought about it, I realized that I had never imagined my life without her in it. It was...unfathomable. Impossible.

"I'm being open and honest with you," I told her. "You have to tell me how to fix this! I love you and I need you and I can't even imagine a life without you in it. Please. How do I fix this?"

There had to be a solution. There just had to be.

Emzee looked away, tightening her arms around her knees.

"You can't fix it," she said. "I just need you to leave."

EMZEE

CHAPTER 11

Morning sickness was the absolute worst.

I had spent the last hour on my knees in front of my toilet, head in my hands, a cold washcloth wrapped around my neck. The waves of nausea and vomiting didn't seem to be letting up anytime soon. I wasn't even sure what I had left to throw up, but every time I thought I was done, another wave had me clinging to the porcelain all over again.

Munchkin let out a whimper of sympathy from the doorway and I told him everything was fine as I squeezed my eyes shut, wondering how I was going to get myself off the floor long enough to get dressed and ready for work, let alone make it into the office at all.

I had been puking almost nonstop from these stupid hormones, but it still couldn't purge all the awful feelings I had about last night and how I'd given Ford false hope that we could make it work. I'd had a weak moment. I'd let him in when I should have stayed firm, should have turned him away. The sex had been explosive, the bond between us undeniable...but it never should have happened in the first place.

Not only had I ripped Ford's heart out and thrown it on the floor, but I had given myself a raging case of the Feels as well.

I thought I had been getting over him—okay fine, I hadn't really thought that, but I thought that I'd been getting *close* to getting ready to get over him—and I'd just completely undermined all that hard work and the distance I'd put between us. Which was frustrating as all hell. The situation we were in was his fault. Mine too, but I'd gone into it with open eyes...or so I had thought. Ford had been the one keeping information from me all along.

I felt a twinge of guilt knowing I was being a hypocrite now, not telling him about the baby. But he had given me no choice. Or, his family had given me no choice.

Why couldn't I just rip the damn Band-Aid off? And why couldn't I stop puking?

I needed to get it together. I was going to be late for work, and the deadline for everything related to *lookingglass*'s very first printed issue was tonight. It would be amazing to hold the magazine in my hands, printed on real paper, the photographs in full color. Not that electronic copies weren't legit, but there was something extra special about having a physical copy to hold on to, to mail to our subscribers, to appear in newsstands and on bookstore shelves.

But I was nowhere *near* ready.

And a sick day was out of the question. Andrew and the whole team were counting on me. As evidenced by the fact that the entire time I'd been throwing up and clinging to the toilet like a lifesaver, my phone had been going nuts, buzzing frantically on the edge of the sink. I was certain when I looked at it, I'd see a stream of texts and emails and calls from my coworkers detailing all the urgent tasks I still had to complete, and wondering where the hell I was.

My phone buzzed again. And again, until it literally fell off the sink and landed on the bathmat beside me. I had a million things to do, and none of them were leaning my forehead against the porcelain and wondering if there were any more saltines in the kitchen as Munchkin came over to lick my elbow.

"I know," I told him. "You're ready for your walk. Just a few more minutes. And then you're going to the doggie spa. I've got a brutal day ahead of me, and I need you out of my hair."

I gave him a scritch and hoisted myself to my feet, all but tossing myself into the shower, letting the cool water refresh me.

After I got dressed, I put Munchkin in his harness and we took a brisk walk to the subway. By the time we got off in Manhattan, I felt a lot better. After I dropped him off at the pet spa a few blocks from work, I arrived at the *lookingglass* offices just in time for the start of the day. Out of breath, I settled myself at my desk, relieved that I'd managed to pull it together.

I booted up my computer to get started, feeling energized and ready to rock.

My productivity lasted all of five minutes before my cell phone rang.

I glanced at the screen, intending to send it to voicemail, but my stomach dropped when I saw that it was Emma. Dammit, I had to pick up. I'd been ducking her calls for weeks now, but I knew that See Yourself couldn't function without its executive director, and that the executive director couldn't run the non-profit when she had no clue what was going on.

"I'm so sorry," I said when I picked up. "Everything's been crazy here."

"I'm just glad I finally got ahold of you," she said, but there was tension in her voice.

I couldn't blame her. I'd been avoiding her ever since I'd skipped town, leaving her in charge of See Yourself while I tried to escape into my new life in New York. She deserved an explanation, but I didn't want to involve her in my personal drama, and I couldn't bear the thought of talking about my divorce—or my pregnancy—to anyone.

At the same time, it was no excuse. I'd left her high and dry right after the charity's hugely successful fundraiser at the Four Seasons. My timing had been shit. With all the good PR we'd gotten and all the donations we'd raised, it was exactly when See Yourself needed a strong leader the most. I'd messed up badly, and now I was going to have to fix it. Somehow.

"Am I to assume that I'm cancelling all your photography classes and one-on-ones with your mentees?" Emma asked dryly. "Or that the fundraiser was such a wild success that we can just fly the women out to New York now?"

There was a tart sarcasm in her voice, but I had earned it.

"No," I said quietly, leaving my cubicle to go hide in a more private corner of the office. "That's not the plan."

"Then did you have a replacement in mind?" she asked. "What do you want me to do? I'm getting calls and emails daily, and all I can tell anyone is that there's been a family emergency that's come up with, because I can't very well admit that you've ghosted the entire charity."

"You're right. I put you in a terrible position. You have

every right to be frustrated and upset with me," I said, trying to keep my voice from wobbling.

I could hardly hold back my guilty tears. I was beyond overwhelmed with everything that had happened in the last month, from leaving my family and moving to New York, to the pregnancy and the surging hormones and nausea, to Ford's now-constant presence and last night's ill-advised fuck session. I could barely keep it together as I tried to soothe Emma.

"I'm not upset with you," she said, sighing. "I'm just worried, and stressed. And yeah, frustrated. This isn't like you. Plus I have no idea what I'm doing here. I'm panicking."

"I'm sorry," I said again, grateful for the note of under-standing in her tone. "I promise I haven't ghosted. I actually *am* dealing with some family issues, but I haven't aban-doned you or my principles or anything like that."

"Are you sure?" she asked. "Because I heard that you started a fancy new job out there, so it's hard not to think you're just focusing all your time and attention on that now. The organization can't run itself. I wish it could, but it doesn't work like that."

"I know. And yes, I do have a new job," I told her. "But I assure you, that's not the reason I've been unavailable. Why don't we go over everything that's on your plate? That way I can have a full plan of action ready to email you by tomorrow."

Even though the thought of "tomorrow" made my stomach clench with dry heaves all over again, because I still hadn't gotten any headway on my to-do list for the magazine. Meaning I wouldn't be sleeping tonight, since I'd have to write up the document for Emma after I clocked out of work, and then it'd be morning and I'd be taking up residence next to the toilet.

After going over everything that See Yourself needed, I was in the process of trying to get Emma off the phone when I got another call. Using it as an excuse to say goodbye, I clicked over —but God, I really, *really* should have let it go to voicemail, because I suddenly had to deal with Mrs. Malone. Someone I had absolutely no time or energy to speak to, even on a good day.

"Why is my son living in New York?" she practically screeched in my ear. "And why the hell hasn't he signed those divorce papers yet?"

For a moment I debated just hanging up on her and hitting decline when she called back...but I knew I couldn't. The next thing I knew, she'd probably show up at my door, or worse—at my job. I might as well just talk to her now and get it over with.

"I can't answer that for him," I told her, exasperated. "I'm just as confused as you are."

"You're responsible for this somehow. I know you are. We had a deal, Mara."

"I know," I said. "And believe me, I'm doing everything I can to follow through with that deal. But I can't control Ford. He found me on his own and moved here on his own. I didn't tell him where I was—I was just as surprised as you were to find out he moved here."

"You always were a sneaky little girl, getting your talons in our boy."

I was glad she couldn't see my eye roll.

"Regardless of what you think is going on, this is *all* Ford," I said. "I've told him in as many ways as I can that we're over, that the marriage is done."

"We're not convinced," Mrs. Malone said.

"I don't know what else to do," I insisted. "I'm trying my best to make this happen."

"Try harder," she said, and then hung up on me.

Using all my willpower to not scream and hurl my phone across the office, I went back to my desk and dropped into my chair, putting my head in my hands. Not even ten a.m., and my entire day had gone to hell. Speaking of which, I had no time to sit here and stew.

When I looked up, I saw Andrew heading toward me. Probably to check on my nonexistent progress. But before I could say anything, the speaker on my desk phone chirped as one of the security guys in the lobby told me that my lunch delivery was on its way up.

Dammit, Ford.

I dropped my head onto my desk with a thump. This was too much.

"Are you okay?" Andrew asked from behind me, sounding worried. "What's up? How can I help?"

I felt his hand on my back, between my shoulder blades, rubbing gently. It felt so nice that I let out a soft little moan.

"It's nothing, I just—" Lifting my head, I turned in my chair and looked up at him. "Honestly, I'm feeling really overwhelmed. And I didn't even *order* delivery, but I think maybe someone just asking me if *they* can help for a change...it kind of helps."

He smiled, and something inside me finally relaxed a little.

FORD

CHAPTER 12

Since all I could think about was Emzee, and given that there was only just so much real estate work I could do for MREH remotely, I decided to direct all my energy into winning her back. There was obviously no point spending all my days in New York inside my apartment just pining for my wife. I had to take action. And I'd come up with a great idea.

Knowing full well that I couldn't get past the security guards at her office without getting the cops called on me, I had to come up with something sneaky. Maybe even a little...underhanded. When it came to wooing Emzee, I was willing to do whatever it took.

My plan was deceptively simple. I ordered lunch takeout—from a Filipino place in the East Village that I knew she'd love—and had it sent to the lobby of her building, where I met the delivery guy. After paying him a hundred dollars cash for his hat and the food, I disguised myself just enough to sneak past the security desk. By now, they were used to seeing so many delivery people coming in and out of the building that they barely paid attention anymore.

Once I got off the elevator on Emzee's floor, the receptionist at the *lookingglass* offices was happy to point me in the direction of my wife's desk. Nobody looked at me twice. In fact, the office was mostly empty, probably because most people were out for lunch.

Excitement rushed through me as I headed past the cubicles, knowing Em would be surprised. The food alone would earn me points; I'd never met anyone who was as much of a dedicated foodie as Emzee. I'd ordered her crispy beef dumplings, crab fried rice with garlic and scallions, and slow roasted pork shoulder in coconut milk. She would love it all.

But when I rounded the corner to her cubicle, the first thing I saw was that shitbird Andrew Apellido, leaning over Emzee and giving her a backrub.

I dropped the food, seeing red. "Get your fucking hands off my wife."

My hands instantly balled into fists. I didn't have to look down to know that there was hot Filipino food all over the floor and my shoes, but I couldn't have cared less. All I cared about was that douchebag and the way he was touching Emzee. I stalked over to her desk and got right up in Andrew's face.

"Didn't I teach you a good enough lesson last time?"

Andrew basically just growled in my face, which did nothing to settle me down in any way. As far as I was concerned, he had another beating coming.

But before I could throw a fist, Emzee had gotten in between us, her hands up. "Stop! What the hell are you doing here?"

"Em—" I tried.

"Get out now, or I'm calling security," she hissed. Turning to Andrew, her voice went calm and placating. "I'm so sorry. I had no idea he was coming here."

What the fuck was this? Soothing words for Andrew and nothing but threats for her own husband? It pissed me off even more. I wanted to tear the guy's dick off and shove it in his ass.

"You need to go," Emzee told me.

I crossed my arms and planted my feet. "I won't."

Emzee's face softened. "Please," she said gently. "Don't make a scene."

Did she think changing tactics and pretending to be nice was going to work? After what I'd just seen? Like hell was I leaving my wife with this opportunistic douchebag.

"I'm not going anywhere," I told her.

"This is my job, Ford," she said, still using that hostage negotiator tone.

"You're my wife."

"Soon to be ex, if you'd just sign the papers," she said.

"Over my dead body."

This was the same argument we'd been having since I'd tracked her down in New York, and we kept going round and round, neither of us budging. This time, however, Andrew was involved—and he kept interjecting, which made me itch to punch him in the fucking face.

"You need to accept that things between us are over," Emzee said.

"Listen to the lady," Andrew added.

I did my best to ignore him.

"You still owe me a discussion," I told Emzee. "Just the two of us."

"There's nothing to talk about," she said.

"The hell there isn't."

"She obviously doesn't want you here," Andrew said, throwing out another verbal jab. "Why don't you take the hint and go."

"Why don't you mind your own fucking business," I told him.

I felt vindicated when he walked away in a huff. Now I could actually have a calm, adult conversation with Emzee. I reached out to her but she sidestepped my hands.

"Are you in love with him?" I asked. "Is that the real reason you came here?"

Suddenly, everything made sense. Why else would she have left Chicago—and me—to move here? So she could work with Andrew. *Be* with Andrew. God, why hadn't I seen it?

Before she could answer me, I realized that Andrew hadn't really left. He'd just gone to get the security guard. And even though I could easily take the kindly older man, I saw that Emzee's eyes were filling up with tears, and that just about broke me. Because it was my fault.

So without putting up a fight, I let the old guy usher me out of the building.

Outside, I paced the sidewalk. I knew I should go. I hadn't even been allowed to stay in the lobby. But there was the bench against the side of the building where I'd waited for Emzee last time, and I sank onto it to give myself a minute to think.

I'd fucked up. Again. Just like I always did with her.

I had meant the lunch delivery to be a fun, romantic surprise...and now it was just a mess for her to clean up, and she was pissed at me all over again. Even more likely to go running into the comforting arms of her sleazeball boss, if that wasn't her intention all along.

If I wanted to win her back, I knew I had to be more

mature about the situation. Had to change my tactics. Head in my hands, I took a deep breath and tried to look at things from her perspective.

First off, I'd intruded on her day, been aggressive with her boss, and possibly had gotten her in trouble with him, with the addition of potentially embarrassing her in front of her coworkers in the process. Even if most of them were at lunch, they'd likely gossip about it later.

Not cool.

I hated the thought of it, but I probably owed Andrew an apology. I definitely owed one to Emzee, but I planned on apologizing to her in a much different way.

Unfortunately, since the only way I could actually apologize to Andrew was to wait for him on the bench outside, that was exactly what I did for the rest of the day. Time passed, my phone battery died, the sky gradually darkened, and then finally business hours were over. But of course Andrew was the type to work late, so it wasn't until almost seven that he emerged from the building. And I was ready for him.

I just hadn't expected to see Emzee walking at his side, which almost made me lose it all over again.

But instead, I took a deep breath, relaxed my hands—which had reflexively clenched into fists—and stood. The minute I did, Emzee's step faltered, and the smile on her face disappeared.

"You waited for me?" she asked, incredulous. "Oh my God, Ford. You can't do this."

I had barely approached them, but Andrew had already stepped in front of Emzee, subtly shielding her from me. Poised to protect her. As if I'd ever hurt my wife.

That piece of shit needed to go, but I knew the best way to get rid of him was to make nice. I could pretend, at least.

"Actually, I was waiting for Andrew," I said.

It wasn't a lie.

"Really," he said, eyeing me skeptically.

"Really. I wanted to apologize."

"For what?" Emzee asked suspiciously.

"For making assumptions about your relationship," I said, even though it was physically hard to actually say it out loud. I knew that Andrew wanted Emzee—I'd known it in my gut ever since the first time I'd met the guy and seen the way he acted toward her—but I couldn't let my jealousy get the best of me now. "And for any trouble I've caused, and for barging into your place of business. Oh, and for the mess I made when I dropped the food up there. I'm happy to pay for floor cleaning and to cover anything else that may have been ruined. I've been an ass."

That part was definitely true.

"Well," Andrew said, clearly taken aback. I could tell he was surprised by the "bigger man" tactic. "I appreciate the apology."

"I appreciate you taking care of her," I said, nodding my head toward Emzee.

When I held out my hand, he accepted the shake warily.

Then he turned to my wife. "I have to rush to a thing. Will you be all right?"

Bristling, I kept my mouth shut. Turning a new corner and all that crap.

"I'll be fine," she said. "I'm just going to pick up Munch from the daycare and then catch a cab home."

Andrew nodded.

"I'll go with you," I said. "So you're not alone."

I half expected her to refuse, but the look in her eyes said I'd just scored a few points.

"Okay," she said. "That sounds good."

We said goodbye to Andrew and then headed down the street.

I'd say it was a solid win for the new and improved Ford Malone.

EMZEE

CHAPTER 13

The whole ride back to Brooklyn—with a freshly groomed Munchkin in my arms, and Ford at my side—I struggled. There was just too much...too much everything.

Too many tasks, too many people who needed me, too many goddamn lies.

But despite all that, I'd somehow miraculously managed to finish all my *lookingglass* work in time for the magazine's debut print issue deadline. And I'd done a damn good job, at that. I had somehow forgotten how buoyed I always felt when I did a good job on something that was important to me. When I made the magic happen.

I snuck a glance over at Ford, quickly looking away when he caught me and smiled. Things felt so upside down, with him doing all the chasing and me running. I was happy, though, that he had come to his senses and apologized to Andrew earlier. After him showing up at my office and making such a scene, I didn't think there was any way he could make amends, but I had been pleasantly surprised by his apology.

Hopefully, someday, he'd find a way to be buoyed by something that was important to him, too. Though I suspected his constant need for his parents' approval probably sucked out any real hope of that.

Then again, he *was* here in New York trying to win me back, instead of in Chicago with his family doing whatever they wanted him to do. Maybe he'd carve his own path after all.

When we arrived at our apartment building, we went inside together silently. It wasn't until we were in the elevator that Ford cleared his throat and glanced at me hesitantly.

"Can I...offer you a drink or something?" he ventured. "I want us to talk. I promise not to get out of hand."

"Umm..."

I was about to refuse, but I realized that this *did* have to be done. Sooner or later, we had to talk. And if I could convince Ford to sign the divorce papers, it would be one more task off my list. Clearly my attempts at shutting him out hadn't been working. Maybe it was time for Plan B.

If I could get this taken care of quickly enough tonight, it might very well give me the energy boost I needed to open my laptop and write up that work email for Emma at See Yourself. Although...there was definitely one other thing that gave me that kind of boost. And my hormones were certainly on board with the idea.

Could I possibly seduce Ford into signing, and kill two birds with one very wicked stone? It was worth a shot. Especially since nothing else had worked so far.

"You know what?" I said. "I've got more work to do tonight, but how about a sparkling water? Just let me drop Munchkin off at my place and then I'll be right up."

He lit up.

"Of course," he said. "I'm ready when you are."

Minutes later, I was knocking on the door to Ford's apartment. I was barely over the threshold before he was apologizing again. He had a glass of ice and a can of La Croix waiting for me on the coffee table. I couldn't help noticing that his place was about twice the size of mine, and it looked like he'd ordered all his furniture from a Restoration Hardware catalogue just to get it furnished quickly. It was nice, just kind of beige and impersonal.

"I'm sorry again, about today," he said. "I know I've been over the top, but I just can't give up on you. On us."

My heart twisted in my chest as I sank onto the couch and poured the water into the glass. I knew I had to stay strong. I couldn't risk getting another case of the Feels. I had to be firm.

"You know you have to," I told him quietly.

He dropped onto the other end of the couch with a sigh. I took a sip of the sparkling water and then slid closer to him.

"I don't have to do anything," he said. "Especially if it doesn't feel right. And this divorce, it doesn't feel right."

"But don't you want to make me happy?" I asked.

I leaned in, and I could see interest flare in his eyes. He seemed to know exactly where this was going.

"Of course I do. I just—"

Before he could say anything else, I grabbed him through his pants. He was already hard and he let out a groan, his cock warm and rock solid against my palm.

"Make me happy, Ford," I whispered.

"Oh, I'm going to make you very, very happy," he said.

Then he pulled me onto his lap and covered my mouth with his.

Both of us had gone far too long without sex, and I

could feel the taut electricity between us as we kissed, aggressive and breathless and unstoppable. I was horny as fuck and desperate for him, tugging his shirt free from his pants so I could slip my hands into his briefs, grabbing his cock and squeezing it.

Ford moaned, thrusting in my grip, and I couldn't help smiling against his mouth. It was hard to believe I'd been a virgin before him. That now I could wield such power.

That power didn't last long.

Once I had Ford's pants down, he took my hand and pulled me off the couch, then led me to the sliding glass doors that opened onto his balcony. He turned the light off so we could see the city lights and then pinned me against the glass.

"Fuck," I gasped. "That's cold."

"I'll have to warm you up then."

Grabbing my hair, he tugged my head back and kissed me ravenously, his mouth everywhere. My lips, my throat, my shoulder, capturing my earlobe between his teeth. The sensation made me moan.

Spurred on, he shoved me harder into the glass, so my nipples were tingling with the cold and friction. He pushed my dress above my hips, dipping a hand down the front of my panties and groaning when he found me wet.

"Is your pussy ready for me?" he growled, pushing his cock against my ass.

"Yes," I said, reaching down to pull my underwear aside and guide him to my entrance. He was still in his button-down shirt, but I was fully dressed—which was fine with me. I didn't want to make this more than what it was: a seduction, and nothing more.

I also didn't want Ford to look at my body too closely. I could tell it was starting to change in small ways, and the last thing I wanted was for him to notice. Getting fucked from behind against a glass door was exactly the kind of sex I was looking for right now.

Which is why when he tried to turn me around to face him, I spread my legs wider and slammed back into him, forcing his cock inside me. He didn't argue, just grabbed my hips and buried himself deeper, making me cry out as he went to work slamming into me, hard and fast. I could see my breath fogging up the view of Manhattan, but nothing else mattered except the feel of him inside me, the mingling of our moans, the rhythm we were finding.

"Yes, yes, yes," I panted. He felt so good, tears were stinging my eyes. "Fuck me."

"Oh my God, oh *fuck*," he was saying over and over, his movements getting jerky and more erratic by the second.

I knew he wouldn't be able to hold back much longer.

Reaching down, I slid a finger over my clit and rubbed myself in little circles as I continued grinding back against Ford's cock.

"Fuck me," I said again. He always loved it when I cursed, when I talked dirty. "Fuck that tight little pussy. Make me come."

Hearing him groaning helplessly as he drove into me was enough to send me over the edge. My orgasm hit, so hard it took my breath away. Ford tightened his arms around me, holding me up as my pussy clenched tight around him. I shuddered, moaning softly with every wave of pleasure, and he finally let himself go, filling me with his hot release.

Even though I could feel his arms trembling from the strain, he held me up against the glass, kissing the back of my neck and shoulders, not willing to let go. I didn't want him to let go, either, which is why I pulled away.

Adjusting my clothes, I walked across the room to my purse, where the divorce papers were. Ford turned around, but his expression hardened when he realized what was in my hands.

"No," he said.

The post-sex glow faded immediately. Seducing him had been my last ditch attempt to get him to sign, but now I was at my wits' end.

"You need to sign," I told him, digging around for a pen.

I needed this, I had a plan for this, and I was sick of his games.

"I won't."

"We're done, Ford. You need to accept that."

"We are so far from done, and you know it," he said. "Why are you doing this?"

"Just sign the damn papers!" I ordered, holding up the pen.

Ford walked over to me, still naked and irritatingly hot. My mouth was watering all over again.

"I love you, Em," he said. "And that's why I'll never sign those fucking papers."

I grabbed my stuff, trying to ignore the way my body was still humming from my orgasm. "Fine. But don't speak to me again," I told him. "This was it. Enjoy the memories."

Then, before he could say anything more, I stormed out of his apartment and went back to mine. My heart was racing in sheer panic as I turned on my laptop to email Emma. What the hell was I going to do now? I needed that divorce. I needed his parents to clear my family's debt to the Bratva. I needed to move on with my life. But Ford was making it absolutely impossible.

My inbox loaded, and of course there was a fresh email from Mother Malone. Fuck.

I was desperate. And desperate times called for desperate measures, didn't they?

Smoothing the folded divorce papers on my desk, I carefully forged the missing signature. After seven years, Ford's handwriting was easy enough for me to copy. I had no other choice. Then, just to make sure I couldn't turn back, I took a picture of the document and emailed it to Mrs. Malone. I included a message.

"Now it's on you to convince him to stop stalking me."

EMZEE

CHAPTER 14

I was woken from a deep sleep to my phone buzzing relentlessly on my nightstand. My first instinct was to roll over and ignore it, but then I realized that it was the middle of the night—and if someone was calling me, it was probably an emergency.

Adrenaline rushing, I grabbed my phone and squinted at the glowing screen.

It was Stefan.

"Hello?"

"Tori's in labor," he said, sounding terrified and excited at the same time.

"Ohmigod!" I said, the shock of the news jolting me fully awake. "I'm coming home! I have to be there!"

"I'll send the jet," he said.

"There's no time for that," I told him, stumbling out of bed and flailing for the light switch. "I'll take the next available flight out of LaGuardia. Just text me the hospital address. I'm on my way!"

I hung up and hopped into a pair of jeans, frantically

throwing clothes into a carry-on bag, and that's when I realized there was a wrinkle in my plans. A wrinkle that was sitting in his dog bed, looking very confused as to why we were both awake in the middle of the night.

Munchkin.

Usually I'd take him with me, but I'd be going straight from the airport to the hospital and dogs were definitely not allowed there. I couldn't just leave him here alone.

I knew what I had to do. I didn't want to do it, but I had no other choice. This was my most logical option and I needed someone I trusted to take care of my fur baby.

Ford answered on the first ring.

"What's wrong?" he asked.

"Nothing's wrong," I assured him. "But Tori went into labor, which means I need to fly home for the baby. Can you watch Munchkin for a few days?"

"No way," Ford said, and my heart sank.

"Okay," I said, trying to remember if the doggie daycare I dropped Munch at sometimes offered longer term boarding options.

"I'm coming with you," Ford said. "I'll get the building manager to take care of him instead. It'll be fine."

Welp. That wasn't the way I'd thought that would go. But I didn't have time to worry about it. It was fine. Ford could do what he wanted. I wasn't traveling with him, though.

I hung up to let him contact the building manager, Louie, while I used a travel app to book a flight. A single ticket, for myself. It was the last open seat on a nonstop leaving in a few hours, at six a.m., so I'd have just enough time to Uber to the airport and get through security before they started boarding. Then I called Andrew.

After apologizing for the late hour, I told him I wouldn't be in that day and explained why. He was incredibly gracious about the whole thing.

With my weekender packed, I threw together a bag of dog food, toys, bowls, and Munchkin's harness, and then walked him up to Ford's apartment. The door swung open before I was even done knocking.

"Are you ready?" he asked. "I'll just drop Munch off with Louie. He's down the hall."

"I'm ready," I said. "I'll head down to the lobby while you take care of that."

Ford took Munchkin and his supplies from me and I booked an Uber in the elevator on my way downstairs. But instead of waiting for Ford, I immediately walked out the door and after about two minutes, I got into the Uber and asked the driver to get me to LaGuardia as quickly as possible. I knew ghosting Ford wasn't exactly fair, but I didn't feel guilty.

Okay, I felt a little guilty. But it was all for the best.

Ford wasn't my family. He didn't need to come with me to Chicago.

Despite my excitement, I managed to conk out for most of the flight, waking up just in time for our descent into O'Hare. All I could think about was what Tori must be going through. And Stefan, who was probably freaking out. Their lives were about to change forever.

It was a thirty minute drive from the airport to Northwestern Memorial, so by the time I got a cab and rushed into the hospital it was almost ten a.m.

"Labor and delivery, please!" I practically yelled at the receptionist, out of breath from running across the parking lot.

"Do you need a wheelchair?" she asked, looking a bit flustered.

"Sorry, no, it's my sister. Victoria Zoric."

I got Tori's room number and rushed up to her floor, scanning the halls for my family.

And there they all were! Brooklyn and Luka were in a waiting room around the corner from Tori, along with Tori's stepmother Michelle. Paper cups of coffee and vending machine snack wrappers littered the table, and Brooklyn had a copy of *Vogue* open on her lap.

Before I could even say hello, I was engulfed in a hug from Brooklyn, whose own pregnant belly was even bigger than the last time I'd seen her. It was a reminder of how much time had passed, and how much I had missed them. And also why I was putting myself through this torture of divorcing Ford. I was doing it to save all of us from the Russian mob.

"You're here!" Brooklyn was saying, rocking me from side to side. I had to extricate myself before my own morning sickness was activated prematurely.

"How is she? Where's Stefan? What are the doctors saying? Did it happen yet?"

"Slow down, Em," Luka said.

"She already had the baby," Michelle said in her southern drawl, grinning.

"She had the baby!" I yelled, punching the air. "I'm an auntie! This is incredible!"

Luka laughed. "Yes you are. Stefan's with them right now."

Michelle added, "And don't worry about Tori. It was a pretty easy labor, the doctor said."

"I hope I get that lucky," Brooklyn murmured, stroking her belly. "The nurses have been taking us into the room to visit in shifts. Tori's tired, but she can't wait to see you."

"And the baby?" I asked, looking between them. "She's...all good? Healthy?"

"She's perfect," Luka said. His voice was awed and reverent, as if the baby was his own. I'd never seen him look so tender. "She's got the Zoric hair, and Tori's blue eyes."

"She really is a beautiful baby," Michelle said. "I still can't believe I have a granddaughter."

"The tiniest little thing you've ever seen, but with these sweet chubby cheeks," Brooklyn added. "I swear she smiled right at me."

I was already blinking back tears, and I hadn't even met her yet.

When it was finally my turn to be brought back, I practically tiptoed into the room. Stefan looked almost as exhausted as Tori, but both of them were glowing. My brother was sitting on the bed next to Tori, smiling down at a little pink bundle in his arms.

"Is she sleeping?" I whispered.

"Yes," Stefan said quietly. "Come and see."

As I crossed the room, the look that Tori was giving him —so full of love and affection—was almost more than my heart could stand.

"Ohmigod," I said, leaning over Stefan to peek at my niece. Brooklyn was right about the chubby cheeks, and the baby had quite the head full of dark hair, and the sweetest rosebud lips. She looked like a doll. "She's a wonder."

It was amazing how tiny this little life was. How small and how precious.

"Isn't she perfect?" Tori asked.

"She is," I agreed easily. "Look at those little fists. She's a fighter..."

Just then, the baby yawned, and then her eyes opened. The second we made eye contact, a wave of emotions washed over me. "Hi there," I whispered to her.

It was totally overwhelming, having her gaze up at me. I was thrilled and excited and weepy too, my eyes filling with tears. It wasn't just the baby, though. It was the fact that I was going to be a mother too, in less than a year. The whole thing seemed so surreal and just as Stefan gently placed the baby in my arms, the door opened and Ford walked in.

What the hell?

I shouldn't have been surprised. He was resourceful, relentless, and rich, and he'd already proven that when he wanted to find me, there was nothing that could stop him. But it was impossible to be truly angry at him with my brand-new niece cradled in my arms.

As I looked at the father of the baby inside of me, and he looked back at me like I was the most beautiful thing he'd ever seen, I suddenly felt like I was going to fall apart. Because I loved him so much, and because I knew our happily ever after could never happen.

There was no point in lying to myself—I wasn't even close to moving on. I was still completely in love with Ford, and learning the truth of what he had done to me in high school hadn't shaken that.

Yes, he'd made mistakes, and yes, I was upset with him. But we'd been best friends for seven years. He was still the first person I called when I needed help. The first person I thought about when I woke up in the morning, the last person I thought about before I went to sleep. He'd told me that he couldn't imagine a life without me in it, and even though I couldn't admit it to him, I felt the same way about Ford. I always had.

What was I going to do?

Tears slipped down my face, and I smiled down at the baby through them. At least I could pretend I was simply crying out of joy over this perfect little life in my arms, and not the utter mess that I'd made of my own.

EMZEE

CHAPTER 15

My sister-in-law Tori had always had perfect timing; being in Chicago for a few days meant I had the perfect opportunity to have a proper sit-down with Emma instead of trying to explain what had been going on with me over email or the phone.

I ended up taking her out to brunch at The Whale for our face-to-face, because I'd desperately missed their lobster and waffles and also because they served decent mocktails. My plan was to just 'fess up and lay it all out for her, giving her an overview of everything related to my divorce and my escape from Chicago. She deserved an explanation, and I knew I had to renew her faith in me if I wanted her to continue running things at the charity in my stead.

She'd be getting a somewhat redacted version of things, though. I still hadn't told anyone—not my coworkers, not my brothers or sisters-in-law and most definitely not Ford—about the pregnancy, and the real reason I'd moved to New York.

As far as I was concerned, no one needed to know. Yet.

For now, the important thing was to focus on making

sure that See Yourself was in a good place. With maternity leave looming in the not-so-distant future, who knew when I'd be able to take over operations again?

"I love working for you, but I can't run the show when you go radio silent," Emma said once we'd settled into a blue leather booth next to the retractable wall of windows. The sun was out, and the window walls were up, letting a cool breeze drift into the restaurant. Despite the tension between us, the ambiance was heavenly.

"I know," I said. "This whole thing was just a giant mess, and I'm so sorry I put you through it."

I gave her a brief rundown then, about how my marriage had crumbled, how my ex refused to sign the divorce papers, how he'd showed up on my doorstep in New York after tracking me there, even though I'd been trying to get away from him. Emma was sympathetic, and she squeezed my hand across the table.

"I'm so sorry. I had no idea. Are you safe?"

"Yeah, it's—he's actually been very sweet. Just...stubborn. I would have told you sooner, but I didn't want to bring my drama to the charity, or dump all this personal stuff on you. Everything's just been falling apart, and it's sort of embarrassing to even have to talk about it."

"Understandable." She nodded. "Emzee, I believe in the non-profit, and I believe in you. That's why I'm still here. But even with everything you've been through, we have to figure out a way to keep things up and running here if you're going to be living a thousand miles away."

Our waiter arrived with our drinks—mimosa for Emma, watermelon juice with non-alcoholic tequila for me—and took our orders. We both got the lobster and waffles, but I added a side of fruit and a side of bacon.

"Someone's extra hungry today," Emma noted.

"Umm, no, I've just really missed this place—and I don't know when I'll be back," I said. It wasn't a total lie.

"I hope that's not true, because we need to talk about rescheduling your photography classes and one-on-one sessions with the mentees," she said, firm but gently. "We can't leave everyone hanging. Unless you want to hire another professional photographer to take over your classes? We can certainly afford it. I've already done some outreach, just in a general way."

"No, I want to do it," I said. "I love working with the girls."

"Great." She pulled out her iPad and day planner and adjusted her glasses, shifting back to the take-no-prisoners Emma that I knew so well. "So I gather you're in New York for good?"

Her brows were raised, her stylus poised over the screen. It was obvious she was still frazzled, but trying to be solution oriented. I couldn't blame her for being anxious. I'd skipped town out of the blue, without so much as a warning to my charity or the people who depended on it. Now I had to smooth things over and figure out a plan. Shutting down wasn't an option.

Even with my life in varying states of upheaval, See Yourself was still the most important thing I'd ever done and it meant the world to me. Providing a support system and a way forward for the women my father had hurt was my way of balancing out his crimes, albeit in a small way.

"I'm in New York for the foreseeable future," I said carefully. "I'm not sure if it's permanent, though."

"Okay. How often do you think you can come back? Quarterly, monthly...?"

I thought on it. It wasn't until I'd seen my family at the hospital that I'd realized exactly how much I was missing them, and my home city. New York was thrilling and chaotic and I loved the challenge and the energy of the place, but I wasn't sure it would ever be home to me.

"I can fly back at least once a month," I told her. "Maybe more, but let's shoot for once a month and see how it goes. I can combine my photo classes into longer weekend workshops and group my mentees into batches, that way I can cover everything when I'm here."

Grabbing my mocktail, I took a healthy swallow, wishing it was the real thing. I didn't mention my upcoming maternity leave to Emma. We'd have to cross that bridge later.

She nodded and made a note. "Perfect. When will you be ready for your first weekend? I want to update the class schedule ASAP and email the girls."

"How about next month? That's only a few weeks away and it'll give us time to plan."

"Love it. Everyone's been asking about you. They miss your classes. And you."

My heart tugged with the memory of how much I enjoyed teaching those classes, and of course, working one-on-one with the women. I got just as much from them as they did from me. I couldn't wait to get back at it.

ONE MORE GOOD thing about being back in Chicago was that I could see my OB/GYN and get my medical files to bring to my new doctor in New York. Thankfully, when I called, my obstetrician was able to squeeze me in for a final appointment at the same time.

Once I got into the exam room, I changed into a gown and lay down on the crunchy white paper covering the examination table. I stared up at the ceiling, heart pounding with nerves as I waited for my doctor to come in.

"How are you feeling, Mara?" she asked once she came in with my chart. "How's the pregnancy been going?"

It was a relief to be able to talk to someone about it.

"It's going okay, for the most part," I said. "But I've had a lot of morning sickness that makes it hard to get to work on time. I expected it, but I didn't realize it would be so bad."

"If you want, I can write you a prescription for an anti-nausea medicine."

"It won't hurt the baby?" I asked.

"No, not at all. But if you're concerned, you can stick to natural remedies. Ginger tea, mint, lemon water. I've also had patients do really well on a regimen of B6 vitamins. It's 25mg, three times a day, and you can get it at any pharmacy."

I made a mental note of my doctor's suggestions, knowing I'd place an online order for all of the above before I flew back to New York.

"I know it seems overwhelming now," my doctor was saying. "But once you get into the second trimester, the nausea usually goes away and you'll feel better. A lot of my patients say their second trimester is the best."

It was a relief to hear.

"Shall we check on baby's heartbeat?" she asked.

"Yes, please," I said, my voice thick with emotion.

I'd been through a lot over the past two days. Not only was I experiencing a whirlwind of emotions after reuniting with my family and meeting my new niece, but I'd also been thrown off guard by the arrival of my own baby daddy. I hadn't heard from Ford since he'd left the hospital. Stefan had been surprisingly kind in asking my ex to leave, and

Ford had complied, looking a little wistful on his way out. It had tugged at me, but I'd had to let him walk away.

The doctor brought in a young technician, and after having gel smeared over my belly, the tech put the transducer on my abdomen and began the ultrasound. I could see a fuzzy black-and-white image on the computer screen, a dark area in the middle where the baby was growing, and to the side, the rate and pattern of its heartbeat. My baby's heartbeat.

"This is your baby," the tech said with a smile, pointing at a curved white blob on the screen. "We're picking up about a hundred thirty-two beats per minute."

"Is that good?"

"It's very strong," my doctor reassured me. "A very good heartbeat."

As I looked at the little bean, I started crying. I was happy, but at the same time it was sad and lonely seeing the baby on the monitor without Ford at my side. It was heartbreaking. The only thing that made me feel better about our breakup was that I'd have his child. Our child. The baby would always be my connection to him, even if I was the only one who knew it.

Of course, I had a fair amount of guilt about keeping the news from him, but I didn't have any other choice. I had to do this for my family. There was no other way. At least, that's what I kept telling myself.

When the checkup was over, the doctor and the tech left me alone to get dressed. My mind was racing. As I put my clothes back on, I couldn't help wondering if I was making the right decision. Was depriving my child of their father really the best thing for my family? It felt like this was another moment—in a long line of moments throughout my life—where I was grappling with the choice to do the Zoric thing, or the right thing.

I walked out of the doctor's office in a haze of confusion and inner turmoil. Collapsing onto a bench outside, it took me a moment to realize that someone was coming toward me.

It was Ford. He'd followed me. And he looked worried.

"What are you doing here?" I asked.

"Seriously?" he asked, gesturing at the sign for the doctor's office, which very clearly had the words obstetrician-gynecologist on it. "What are *you* doing here? Is something wrong? Why are you seeing an OB/GYN here in Chicago?"

He knelt down in front of me, looking up into my eyes with concern and love. My defenses were down. I didn't have the energy to lie anymore.

I took Ford's face in my hands, inhaling deeply.

"I'm pregnant," I said.

FORD

CHAPTER 16

Emzee was pregnant.

My wife was fucking pregnant!

Joy surged through me.

"We're going to have a baby?"

"I am," she said softly.

Wrapping my arms around her, I murmured, "My God. When? How far along are you?"

"About two months."

"Two months!" I yelled. I was fucking ecstatic.

Until I did the math. And then suddenly, the reality of our situation sunk in.

I pulled away. "Why didn't you tell me you suspected something? I would've come to the appointment too, been with you when you found out."

Her silence said it all. This hadn't been a confirmation. She'd already known.

"Jesus Emzee, how long have you known for?"

She just shrugged, looking down at the ground, which only served to piss me off more. What the hell was going on? Had she known about the baby when she ran away to

New York? What about every time she harassed me to sign the divorce papers—had she known then, too?

Frustrated, I started pacing the sidewalk outside the doctor's office. It was a warm day, and I was sweating in my blazer. "When were you planning on telling me about this? Or were you not?"

"Ford," she said, her voice quiet.

"Em." I shook my head as if I was waking up from a dream. Because that's how this whole thing felt. Like it was a dream. Or a nightmare. I couldn't tell.

I was thrilled about the baby, but furious that she had kept it from me.

"How could you not tell me?" I demanded. "This is our baby. Our child. Did you think you were going to raise the kid in secret? I would have found out sooner or later."

Questions were tumbling out of me all at once. I needed answers. My whole world had just been upended.

Emzee cleared her throat. "I've known for about a month," she confessed.

I let that information sink in, and I wasn't happy. "So you knew you were pregnant when you asked for a divorce. You knew when you left Chicago," I said, feeling sick to my stomach. "And you never said anything."

"That night of the gala, I took a pregnancy test. That's when I knew," she said, lifting her chin stubbornly. "It was the same night I found out what you did to me in high school."

"So you thought you'd just, what, hide out in some other city for the rest of your life to avoid me and try to be a single parent? Or pretend the kid was someone else's? Maybe get Andrew to play daddy? Do you realize how fucking unreasonable that is?"

"I didn't plan this!" she shouted, getting off the bench to

stand in the path of my pacing. "I'm still trying to figure it all out. I don't know where I'm going to be or what I'm going to do. This is all new territory for me."

She was angry, too. Breathing hard and glaring at me.

"We're not getting a divorce," I said. "We're not over. Not with a baby on the way."

"The baby has nothing to do with what is going on between us," Emzee argued and I wanted to laugh. Because what the hell *was* going on between us? I still couldn't figure it out. The way she jumped from crossing state lines to run away from me to seducing me in my own apartment to throwing divorce papers in my face had given me more than enough whiplash.

It felt like she was slipping away, even though she was standing right in front of me.

"I love you," I reminded her. "The past was a long time ago, and I'm sorry. I fucked up. Let me fix it. Let me fix *us*. I have faith in our relationship, and I know we can be okay again."

She shook her head and I began to feel hopeless, until I remembered the whole reason I had followed her today.

"Wait a minute," I said, and then pulled out my phone, scrolling through my messages until I found the one I'd gotten from my parents. "What the fuck is this nonsense about me signing the divorce papers? My parents are already trying to set me up on dates."

I shoved my phone at her. At the picture my parents had sent of some random girl.

Emzee frowned. "Who is that?"

"I have no idea," I told her. "But I'm sure she won't be the last mystery date they set me up with, because apparently I'm now legally divorced. You know anything about that?"

The color drained from Emzee's face. My stomach dropped to my feet.

"Emzee," I said. "What did you do?"

"I...sort of forged your name on the papers," she admitted.

Mind blown, all I could do was laugh, even though I was seeing red. "You did what?"

"You refused," she argued. "I couldn't keep waiting."

Sinking back down on the bench, I put my head in my hands. I couldn't believe what I was hearing. Then I looked up at her again.

"You forged my name and hid a pregnancy?"

"Yes. I did."

The ground felt like it was actually tilting beneath my feet. I tried to take a few deep, calming breaths to fight the vertigo. This could not be happening. This was not my life.

"First of all," I told her. "There is no way in hell you're getting rid of me when you're pregnant with my child. Secondly, that signature is not legal, and I'll contest it. And win. You know I will. I know some great lawyers."

"Ford, don't—" she started to say, but I held up my hand to silence her.

"I don't want to hear it. I can't be around you right now."

No matter how much I loved my wife, I couldn't stand the thought of being with her for one more second. I was too pissed. Too hurt. It was painful enough that she'd walked out on me and moved to New York on the sly, but the fact that she hadn't told me about the baby—our baby—had shattered something inside of me. My chest ached. I needed some time alone to process everything.

"How could you do this to me?" I asked quietly. "How could you keep this a secret?"

"You had secrets too," Emzee said, her voice taking on an edge. "And you kept them from me for years."

I couldn't believe she was comparing the two. Okay, sure, I knew that the whole modeling/prostitution ring was a big deal, and yeah I should have come clean ages ago about the locker graffiti and the whore rumors I'd started about her, but God, that was so long ago. It was in the distant past. Whereas this, all this with the baby and the divorce and the New York stuff, this was happening right now. It was the present *and* the future. Our future. Baby's future.

"This doesn't even begin to compare," I told her. "And you know it."

I stood up and started pacing again, unable to help myself. I didn't know what to do or say, and it was clear that Emzee didn't either. How had our lives become so messed up so quickly? And how could we ever make things right again? For our baby's sake if nothing else.

Finally, I walked back over to her and took a deep breath. I'd made my decision.

"This is my child," I told her. "And I love you, Em."

She looked up at me with a big, questioning stare. "What happens now?"

"I honestly don't know. But no matter what happens, we're going to figure this out. Somehow. Together," I said, measuring my words carefully. "As for today, right now, I'm going to fly back to New York and take some time and space for myself. Let me know when you're in Brooklyn again, and I'll see you there. And Emzee?"

"Yes?"

"Please don't run away from me again. Promise me."

Slowly, she nodded. "I promise."

EMZEE

CHAPTER 17

I didn't stay long in Chicago. As much as I wanted to spend time with my family and my newborn niece, I had restarted my life in New York and I couldn't just abandon that as well. After one more day visiting with my brothers and sisters-in-law at the hospital, I hurried back to New York—to the city, to my job at *lookingglass*, to Munchkin.

At least my dog still loved me.

I had thought that throwing myself into the new life I'd built would be enough to keep my mind off everything. The daily hustle of the magazine and my photographs and Munchkin's pupcakes. All the things that used to distract me and make me feel fulfilled. But as it turned out, I couldn't outrun my conscience.

And I couldn't erase the memory of Ford's face when he found out that I was pregnant, and that I'd hidden it from him. I felt like a villain.

After spending so many nights blaming him for everything that had gone wrong in my life, I was now grappling with the fact that I had become the bad guy in *his* life. It wasn't just the morning sickness that was making me nauseous these days. Even if my big plan to hide the baby's parentage had gone off without a hitch, I'd been planning to make choices that were bound to hurt him. In addition to the ones I'd already made.

When I initially fled Chicago, I'd been certain I was doing the right thing for everybody: myself, the baby, Ford, the entire Zoric family. Now, I wasn't so sure. Because long before I started blaming Ford for betraying me, I had loved him. Without reservation. In fact, if someone had asked me a year ago if there was anything Ford could do to shake my loyalty, I would have said no. Not a chance. But that was before I found out just how much he was hiding from me.

And yet. Even after everything he'd put me through, there was no doubt in my mind that I still loved him.

God, what had I been thinking? Did I really think he wouldn't ever find out the baby was his? Or had part of me secretly hoped that he would, and that he'd end up being the one person in my life that I couldn't push away or hide from? Was it some kind of test I'd sprung on him unawares that I was subconsciously hoping he'd pass?

Truly, if there was a Zoric family curse, it was fucking up with the people they claimed to love. I'd messed things up with Ford in so many ways. There was only one thing to do—come clean. About everything. Including the Bratva and my deal with his parents. As hard as it was going to be, the thought of getting everything off my chest was a huge relief.

The last time I'd seen Ford, outside my doctor's office in Chicago, he'd said that we would figure things out together, and to let him know when I was back in Brooklyn. I didn't know if he'd meant figuring out the marriage or just having some real talk about the divorce and the custody of our eventual child, but when he'd walked away from me, he'd been holding back a lot of hurt and anger. I knew him well enough to be certain of that. He'd also said that he needed some space, which was part of the reason why I'd been avoiding him since my return to NYC. Of course he'd needed to process, and stew, and think it all over. I had, too.

But now it was time to face him.

My mind was made up. I'd go straight to his place after work. He'd given me a key to his apartment last month, so I'd just let myself in and wait for him if he wasn't there. I'd camp out on the couch and make him listen, refuse to leave until he heard me out. I'd insist we be fully honest with each other and figure everything out once and for all. Together. For better or worse.

I'd show Ford I could be just as stubborn as he could.

After dropping Munchkin off at my place, I popped back out to the hipster liquor store up the street to pick up some grapefruit Perrier for me and a bottle of Ford's favorite bourbon, since a little well-meaning bribery never hurt anybody. When I got to his apartment, I went over to the bar immediately, first pouring myself some water to calm my stomach and then setting the Pappy Van Winkle next to the almost finished bottle already there.

I had just settled onto the couch when I heard a voice coming from the other room. Toward the back of the apartment. It was a woman's voice.

"Back so soon?"

The last time I'd been over, we hadn't left the living room area. I'd never seen the rest of his place, but I had a sense that the voice was coming from where the bedroom was. My stomach turned as I moved through Ford's apartment, feeling like an interloper, afraid of what—or who—I would find.

Following the direction of the voice, I found Ford's bedroom—along with the person I wanted to see least in the world. Claudia.

In Ford's bed. In lingerie.

I froze in the doorway, words escaping me. The shock and upset made my mind go blank, just like it always did, just like back in high school whenever I was harassed or catcalled or cornered by mean girls with sharp tongues who were exactly like Claudia and her friends.

Our eyes met, and for once, Claudia didn't say anything either. Not that she had to. It was clear to both of us that she'd already won.

Claudia sat up straighter on the bed, her sculpted body barely contained by the pale pink lace lingerie she was wearing. Her lips curved into a mean little smile, and she tossed her long blonde hair back. With that smile, I was completely undone.

I ran.

Flinging open the front door, I found Ford standing there, key in his hand. Of course I had to bump into him on my way out. As if I could ever manage a clean getaway when Ford Malone was involved.

"Emzee," he said, sounding pleasantly surprised.

"*You*," I replied, practically spitting the word.

My eyes were tearing up, still burning with the image of Claudia sprawled across his sheets, that cruel, gloating smile of hers. A smile I knew all too well.

I didn't care that Ford looked glad to see me—it was too little, too late for that.

When he'd said he needed space, cheating on me with his vile ex-girlfriend was the last thing I imagined he needed that space for.

At least I no longer felt guilty about what I'd done to

him. As far as I was concerned, Ford's actions only proved that I had made the right choice when I'd run away from Chicago. That not telling him about the baby, and yes, even forging his signature so we could get divorced, had been the right thing. I didn't feel bad about any of it anymore, because Ford had just proven, without a doubt, that I couldn't trust him.

All those sweet words about being in love with me and wanting us to be together and being unable to let me go, they had all been just that—words. *Lies.*

Ford didn't want me. Not really. He only ever wanted what he couldn't have, and so the second he was certain I'd make myself available to him again, just like I always had, he'd run right back into Claudia's arms.

All my guilt over what I'd done evaporated completely.

Ford's expression of happiness morphed into confusion as I pushed past him and stormed into the hallway.

"Em?"

I turned around.

"Fuck you," I said, my voice cold as ice. "We're done. We can fight about custody in court."

FORD

CHAPTER 18

The slam of the door seemed to echo in my ears as I stood in the entryway of my apartment, wondering what the fuck had just happened.

I had no idea why Emzee had just run off like that, clearly pissed off at me and talking about future custody battles. What was even more frustrating was that I'd thought we were finally on the same page. After I got back to New York and spent some time alone trying to clear my head, I'd realized that I already knew exactly what I wanted. It was the same thing I'd been wanting for a while —*her*. I wanted to be with my best friend forever, for real. No fake relationship, no fake wedding, no fake marriage. I wanted us to build a life and a family together. I was determined to make it happen, no matter what it took. That's what I'd been readying myself to tell her.

And instead I came home to...that.

What was she so angry about?

I'd told her I'd need some time to myself, and that she should reach out when she returned to Brooklyn. Had she been waiting for me to make the first move instead? Was it a miscommunication that had gotten blown out of proportion? Why was it always one step forward, two steps back with her lately? It was like I couldn't get off her shit list no matter how hard I tried. Regardless, I wasn't going to let another little tiff come between us. It was time for me to lay it all out. Spill my guts. Tell her how I really felt, and commit myself to her and the baby going forward. After today, we'd only be stronger.

I had to go after her.

Just as I was about to run out the door, the floor creaked behind me. I turned around, and what I saw stopped me in my tracks. There it was. There was the problem.

Fucking Claudia. In some ridiculous pink lace getup with a garter belt and strappy things hanging off it. She may as well have been naked for all it covered.

"Hello, lover," she purred, crawling from the bedroom toward me on her hands and knees.

I knew she was trying to be seductive, but it had zero effect on me.

"What the fuck are you doing here?" I demanded.

Emzee's response—the cussing and the door slamming—made perfect sense now.

Claudia was on her knees now, her lower lip, which was stained with a deep red lipstick, stuck out in a pout. "I'm here for *you*," she said.

"Funny, because I sure as hell didn't invite you here," I said, getting more irritated by the minute. "How did you even get in?"

But even as I asked it, I had a pretty good idea.

"Your mother gave me a key," Claudia said, confirming my suspicions. "She thought it would be a sweet surprise for me to be waiting for you when you got home."

Of course. It all made sense now. I should have known

my mother was up to something when she had been so insistent that I make her a copy of my apartment key while I was in Chicago. I had thought she was being way over the top, even for her, especially since my parents didn't have a place in New York and rarely left Chicago, but now it was clear that she'd fully intended to give the key to Claudia all along.

"There's nothing less sexy than my mom being involved with this," I said. Not that I had found anything sexy about my ex for a long time. "Did she choose your outfit, too?"

"Oh, come on," Claudia stood and walked down the hall toward me, grabbing my shirt and trying to pull me close to her.

I peeled her hands off me and put some distance between us.

Claudia pouted. "Tell me what you want, then. We used to communicate well, Ford."

"Did we?"

She wasn't entirely wrong. We used to communicate well. And we used to have a "good" relationship, the kind where we both had our wants and needs met. But that's because our wants and needs back then were *shallow*. The whole relationship was shallow. There'd never been much to communicate about beyond which parties we'd go to, where to take our next vacation, who to invite out to dinner at some place we'd all brag later about being able to secure a VIP reservation for.

I tried to remember what it had felt like to be with Claudia, if we'd ever talked about anything of substance, or discussed a future that involved something more important than which bougie neighborhood in Chicago we saw ourselves living in or how many figures we thought our salaries would be in ten years. The only memory that stood out to me was how upsetting it was when things didn't work out in the end, but now that I really thought about it, I couldn't recapture that feeling.

Compared to how I felt about Emzee and our unborn child, everything I'd ever had with Claudia seemed dim and small. I think some part of me had always felt that way—that Emzee was the center of my universe. It just took me way too long to figure it out. And now I'd have to make it clear to her as soon as fucking possible.

"You need to go," I told Claudia. "I have somewhere to be."

She frowned. "We don't *have* to have sex," she said. "That was a bonus. You want this to be an appearance-only marriage? Fine with me."

"Claudia—"

"Though that would be a shame," she interrupted, lowering herself back to her knees in front of me. "We did have some good times, didn't we, Ford? All those sexy little encounters we had on our trips around the world? The times we'd sneak a quickie in the hotel hot tub or hurry back to our room to ravage each other after a night of drinking nothing but champagne?"

I almost laughed at the way she was talking about our sex life. Because those anecdotes all seemed ridiculously boring now that she was going on about them. And they paled in comparison to everything I'd done with Emzee. If my wife was all soft curves and sweet gasps and hot dirty talk, then being with Claudia was like fucking a silicone sex doll. All painted up and flashy, but with no life or emotion underneath.

Sex with Emzee? Mind-blowing. Every time.

Screwing her on the roof of that art gallery for one, when anyone could have caught us. Or the time we'd hate-fucked on the desk I'd bought with Claudia in Paris. Or the night Em had seduced me to try to get me to sign the divorce papers, ramming her from behind up against the sliding glass doors, the city lights of Manhattan glowing at us across the river. All of it was hotter than anything Claudia and I had ever done. Hotter than anything I'd ever even imagined.

Unfortunately, Claudia was still talking. I got the feeling that a satisfying sex life wasn't high on her list of priorities for a good marriage.

"We have so much in common," she was saying. "And we have history. Our lives are already so intermingled—our parents are friends, we have the same social circle—getting married would make everyone happy. And if we combine our personal and professional networks, we'll be unstoppable. Plus you know how well we work together."

I didn't want to listen, but she was making some valid points. Our relationship hadn't been full of the same heat and passion I had with Emzee, but it had also been free of the nonstop drama. Em and I fought constantly, and even though we usually made up in a spectacularly hot fashion, it was exhausting. When Claudia and I fought, which was rarely, all I had to do was buy her some jewelry that she could wear and show off to her friends, and all would be forgiven.

Claudia was still listing all the pros our marriage would have: "We both know how to be important, we're ambitious, we have compatible goals, we've already agreed on where we'll live and what we'll do until we retire. Come on, Ford, how does this not make sense to you?"

It did make sense. Our families got along great—and admittedly, it would be nice not having to fight with my parents all the time because I was married to someone they didn't like. And they *loved* Claudia. If I married her, I'd probably earn enough Good Son points to last the rest of my life. They might even trust me to completely take over Malone Real Estate Holdings. With Claudia on my arm, I'd be able to go anywhere, do anything I wanted. Every opportunity I desired would be available to me. We'd be the envy of Chicago.

"Come on, Ford," Claudia begged, reaching her hands out to me. "Say yes."

I imagined—for a second—what my life would be like if I submitted to the future that my parents and Claudia wanted for me. How much easier it would be to let Emzee walk out of my life. I didn't have to chase after her. I could let the divorce be finalized and see my baby on weekends and during the summer.

It would certainly make my parents happy.

But that future I imagined was fleeting, because when I thought about a life without Emzee, I ached.

Being with Claudia was easy. There were no blow-ups. But that also meant there were no challenges to be had. No rewards. No sense that we were pushing each other to greater heights, that the sum of us together was greater than what we could be separately. Those were all things I had with Emzee. Emzee who was also my best friend.

I didn't want to marry Claudia and go back to the life I used to have. I needed the passion I had with Emzee, and if that came with drama, then so be it.

I had to make things right. Starting with kicking Claudia out of my life for good.

She was still kneeling on the floor, arms reaching toward me. The expression on her face indicated that she thought she'd won. That she'd managed to convince me we belonged together.

"We're done," I told her. "You need to leave."

Her mouth dropped open. "What?"

Claudia never did know how to take no for an answer. If I was going to get rid of her, I knew I had to be firm. There had to be no question that whatever had existed between us was over. For good.

"Whatever my mother tells you, this isn't happening," I said. "We're not getting back together and we're not getting married. It's over. It's been over for a long time."

I considered telling her that Emzee was pregnant—that there was now a baby in the equation. Because I knew for a fact that Claudia would die before she'd volunteer to be a stepmother. But I didn't want to use my child like that.

"I've moved on with my life," I add. "It's time for you to move on with yours."

Claudia finally stood up, her hands on her hips. "You can't be serious. You're not really going to choose her over me. I mean, come on. Look at me."

I did. I gave her a long, hard look.

"I've already chosen her," I said. "And I'll *always* choose her. What's it going to take to get through to you? I don't want you."

The predatory gleam seemed to go out of her eyes, her shoulders slumping just a little.

"You're going to regret this," she practically spit at me, eyes narrowing.

I was tired of talking about it. I'd told her in every way I could think of that we were through. I was done, and I wanted her gone.

I could see into my bedroom behind her, and I spotted her suitcase, open on the floor, her clothes spilling out onto the rug. I stalked past her, into the room, and started shoving her things back inside.

"What are you doing?" Claudia said, following me.

It finally seemed to occur to her that I was actually serious. That I wanted her to leave.

"I'm throwing you out," I said, zipping the suitcase and picking it up. "And I want my key back before you leave."

She crossed her arms stubbornly, but I scanned the room and saw a key sitting on my dresser. Claudia saw me notice it, but I grabbed it before she could and shoved it into my pocket.

"I'm not leaving," she said, practically stamping her feet.

"Yes, you are," I told her and grabbed her arm.

I didn't care that she wasn't wearing clothes, that her whole damn body was on display for anyone who might pass by. I dragged her out of my bedroom, one hand on her arm, the other holding her suitcase, and dumped her into the hallway. Then I dropped her bag and shut the door to my apartment behind me.

As I locked it, I heard a loud squeal of annoyance from the hallway. I ignored it.

Claudia must have finally understood what I was telling her, because the next time I popped my head out into the hallway, it was empty.

She was gone.

I'd never felt better.

EMZEE

CHAPTER 19

When I stormed out of Ford's apartment, it didn't occur to me for a second to head back to my own place. Instead, I marched straight out of the building and down the street, not slowing down until I found myself in the Prohibition Era-themed cocktail lounge on the corner. It was the perfect place to curl up in a booth and brood. Nothing but dim lights, dark wood, exposed brick, and pressed tin ceiling tiles as far as the eye could see. It was also pleasantly uncrowded this early in the evening, with maybe a dozen people total.

Sidling up to the bar, I looked up at the chalkboard menu.

That was when it hit me all over again—I couldn't drink.

But no one could stop me from sitting at the bar and having the same kind of good think I'd be having if I *was* able to order one of the cleverly named concoctions.

"Welcome. What can I get you?" the bartender, a cute tattooed guy wearing a period-appropriate hat and suspenders, asked me.

I glanced at the menu again, wishing so badly that I could order a Bee's Knees or a Hanky Panky or even the Sweet Fallen Angel. Pretty much everything was made with gin. Alas.

"Can I just get a soda with lime, please?" I asked.

The bartender made the kind of face that said, "if you're not drinking, why are you taking up a bar stool?"

After everything I'd just been through, I wasn't about to be intimidated by this asshole. So I smiled, exactly the kind of smile Claudia would use to get her way—playful, flirtatious, and with just a hint of apology—and crooked my finger at him in a "come hither" gesture.

It worked like a charm. He leaned over the bar, closer to me.

"I really, really want to try one of these drinks," I told him. I might have even batted my eyelashes a little.

"But...?" he said, clearly interested in my answer.

I pouted. "But I'm still on antibiotics for this sinus infection I'm getting over, and the two don't mix." There was no way I was telling him about being pregnant, not with all the questions that might entail (or worse: pity). "But since I'm just dyyyyying for a drink, I thought I'd do a good deed and pay for the next round for everyone else sitting at the bar. Anonymously, of course."

His eyes lit up and he straightened. "Of course," he said. "I totally get it."

Placated, he made me my soda first and then got orders from the other people at the bar. Then he came back in front of me to mix them all. He was showing off for me, flipping the bottles he poured from and shaking the cocktail shaker like he was in a movie.

As he continued to perform, I smiled at him, grateful for the distraction. But even as I looked on, I was drifting off in my mind. To the reality I couldn't deny I had made for myself.

This divorce was really going to happen, I was really going to be a single mom, and it was really looking like Claudia was going to be my baby's stepmother. Thank God I'd already had years of practice holding back my intense dislike of her behind bland smiles.

I felt like such an idiot thinking that Ford had actually changed. Believing him when he said he loved me and wanted to build a family. I should have known better.

The bar wasn't crowded, which is why I was surprised when a man slid into the seat right next to mine. There were plenty of stools available farther down. Stirring my soda and lime, I hoped I wasn't about to get hit on. I really wasn't in the mood.

Out of the corner of my eye, I could see that he was built like a brick house, overly large for the suit he was in and straining the fabric in the shoulders and arms. It was an expensive suit, though, and it impeccably matched the flashy Ferragamo shoes he was wearing.

"What are you drinking?" the man asked.

Damn. Called it. I turned toward him and noticed that he wasn't bad looking. Not that it mattered. I wasn't in the headspace to entertain revenge-flirting at the moment.

"Just a soda and lime," I said, trying to give off a polite but disinterested vibe.

"Would be better with a little...Stolichnaya," he suggested. "Mind if I join you?"

Making a big show of looking at my watch, I said, "I'm flattered, but I've actually got to run soon. I'm not really looking for company."

Just then the bartender came over, and my new friend ordered a Stoli on the rocks. The bartender poured it out in front of Mr. Stoli, who was quick to take an appreciative gulp before slapping a hundred dollar bill on the bar.

"We'd like some privacy," he told the bartender, who took the money and sidled as far away down the bar as possible.

What the hell?

"I should really be going," I said.

The man smiled. "Few things in life are better than good vodka and good company."

"Right. Well, enjoy it. The vodka, I mean." I tried to sound chirpy as I started to ease off my stool, but before I could get my feet on solid ground, his hand clamped around my upper arm. I stiffened immediately. "Let me go."

"We need to talk," he said, his voice low.

It wasn't a request. It was a threat.

He tugged the lapel of his jacket aside so I could see the black grip of what had to be a handgun tucked into a holster under his arm. Then he raised his brows to make sure I understood, because I'd obviously been a little slow on the uptake.

Nodding carefully, I settled back on the stool.

"Good girl," he said.

I'd been too distracted before to notice that this was not a guy who'd walked into a bar to flirt. Too self-absorbed in my personal pity party to be suspicious when he took an immediate interest in me. But everything was clicking now.

The reason his suit was so tight was because he was packing a lot of muscle under there. A *lot* of muscle. His choice of vodka—a very obvious Russian brand—and the fact that he'd just flashed a weapon at me were all obvious signs: he worked for the Bratva.

Which meant that he was sitting next to me for a reason.

And it couldn't be a good one.

Adrenaline rushed through me, and I could feel my armpits start to prickle with nervous perspiration. It wasn't just my life at stake right now—it was my baby's. Not to mention, my entire family. I had no idea what this guy wanted, and no idea how to handle him. I was fucking terrified. But I knew panicking wouldn't accomplish anything.

Luckily, I was well practiced at disguising my feelings, navigating stressful situations, and keeping my composure around powerful men. And beyond the mandatory etiquette lessons that had been forced on me as a child, I'd spent years honing my survival skills.

My instincts quickly took over.

Rolling my eyes theatrically at him, I said, "Fine. You win. Why don't you get another drink and grab us a booth? I'm going to the ladies' room," slurring my words just enough to seem convincing.

Before he could respond, I got up, making a point to stumble a little on my way across the room, knowing that he was watching me. I had to appear drunk, like someone who might take an extra-long time in the bathroom.

But the moment the bathroom door closed, before the stall was even locked behind me, I had my phone in my hand.

I tried to think fast. Who could I call? My first thought was Stefan, but he was in another state and he'd just had a fucking baby. The last thing I wanted to do was ruin his new daddy glow by telling him that some meathead from the Russian mob had cornered me in a bar.

So I called Luka instead. He wasn't in the same state either, but maybe he would know what to do. He'd definitely been in a lot more shady situations in his life than Stefan ever had.

"He *what?*" my brother practically shouted when I told him about the guy at the bar and how he'd flashed his gun at me.

"He kept it inside his jacket," I told him. "I'm fine."

"Jesus, nothing about this is fine!" Luka said. "We need to get you out of there. Can you call the cops?"

I sighed. "Even if they show up in time to arrest the guy, which I doubt, it'll just make things worse for us later. They'll keep sending people. It's the *mob*, Luka."

"Okay okay okay," he said. "We can figure something out. Let's just think this through."

"Luka, we don't have time! I can't hide in this bathroom forever—he's bound to get suspicious and come after me. There's nothing you can do from Chicago."

We both knew it. So instead of listening to him spitball ideas, I made him promise not to tell Stefan and then hung up and scrolled through my contacts, looking for the only other person I knew in the city who wouldn't be put out at having to rescue me out of the blue. Andrew.

"Emzee, what's up?" Andrew asked when he picked up the phone.

"I'm in trouble," I told him. "Like, code red, nine-one-one emergency-level trouble, except I can't actually call the police."

"Okay," he said calmly. "Where are you?"

I couldn't give him the specific details—i.e., that I was being followed by the Russian mob—but I did tell him which bar I was at and that a real creep had been hitting on me and was *possibly* armed and wouldn't take no for an answer.

"So I need to get out of here, stat," I finished.

Thankfully, Andrew had a plan.

"I know the bar you're at. There's a back door past the

bathrooms that opens into the alley, so you need to sneak out that way and then hang a right toward Metropolitan. About three doors down, you'll see a place called Café Cuba that has a rear entrance. Grab a table in there, by the kitchens, and I'll text you when I pull into the alley. You can duck right into my back seat."

"Got it. Thank you."

"Don't worry. I'll make sure you get home safe."

When I got to the café, I called Luka, who stayed on the phone with me until Andrew arrived. As we drove back to my place, I couldn't stop thinking about the baby...and how much danger my whole family was in. We had to find a way to pay off the Bratva, and fast.

Our lives depended on it.

FORD

CHAPTER 20

Although I wanted nothing more than to take a scalding hot shower and wash every last trace of Claudia off my skin, I knew it wouldn't be enough to rid the apartment of her—I'd have to clean the rest of the place as well. The bedding she'd been half-nakedly writhing on (and God only knew what else)—sheets, pillowcases, and a duvet that Emzee had bought—all went immediately into the laundry. The bathroom got thoroughly bleach sprayed and scrubbed top to bottom, all the floors were Swiffered within an inch of their lives, and I Lysoled every room just to be sure any remnants of my ex's unwelcome visit were neutralized. If I was the woo-woo type, I would have burned sage, but I settled for lighting an ocean breeze scented candle I'd brought from Chicago. It was Emzee's favorite, and the smell reminded me of her.

Once I felt like everything was clean enough, I finally took that shower so I could feel completely rid of Claudia, even though she'd barely touched me. Then I dressed as fast as I could and headed downstairs to talk to Emzee. I needed to explain what had just happened, and we still had to sit down and have the Talk about our lives and our future together. There would be zero hesitation on my part. I didn't care what my parents wanted—especially after my mother had meddled by sending Claudia to New York, which had been a complete, unmitigated disaster. I knew what I wanted. I just had to hope Emzee wanted the same thing.

Outside her apartment, I dug out my keyring, but then hesitated. I had a key to Emzee's place, but I knew I was already on thin ice with her thanks to the whole Claudia thing...it seemed unlikely that barging in unannounced would help matters. So I decided to knock instead. Let Em be the one to decide if she wanted to let me into her space. Or not.

I held my breath, waiting for her to come to the door, my adrenaline pumping. Seconds passed that felt like minutes. Maybe she hadn't heard me the first time. I knocked again.

From inside, I could hear Munchkin's muffled barks, Emzee's voice hushing him, and then it quieted. She was probably putting him in his kennel so she could answer the door.

But when it finally opened, I had to take a step back to prevent myself from swinging.

Because none other than Andrew fucking Apellido was standing there. In his goddamn polo shirt and khakis, with his stupid blonde hair and egregiously chiseled chin.

My blood was up, and all reason fled my brain as I stared him down. What the hell was with this guy? Did he have some kind of fucking sixth sense? He was always lurking around Emzee like a vulture after she and I had a fight, like he just couldn't wait to swoop in and be her rebound. It took every ounce of self-control I possessed not to punch him right in his smug fucking face. Again.

But I had made a promise to Emzee that I wouldn't hurt Andrew again or drag him into our shit. So instead of attacking him, I pretended he wasn't there. Over his shoulder, I could see Emzee sitting on the couch, arms folded over her chest, looking right at me. Okay then. Time to do this.

Pushing Andrew aside as politely as fucking possible, I stormed into the apartment and redirected my anger toward my wife.

"What the hell is going on between the two of you?" I demanded, gesturing behind me at where I assumed Andrew was still standing.

Emzee stood and faced me, her anger matching mine.

"I'm pretty sure that's none of your business," she said.

"I'm pretty sure you're still my fucking wife," I reminded her. "Unless you'd rather be with Andrew. Because it seems like you always run straight to him whenever we have a problem."

Emzee laughed coldly. "Well, that shouldn't be an issue going forward, because I don't expect any future problems with you once the divorce goes through!"

"Over my dead body," I said. Because with a forged signature on those divorce papers, I sure as hell didn't consider us divorced.

"We are *definitely* over," she insisted. "And what do you care about who I'm friends with anyway? It's obvious you'd rather be with Claudia."

"*Fuck Claudia*," I said with passion. "You know as well as I do that she's a conniving bitch. You see her in my apartment looking ready to pounce and you automatically assume the worst? Did it ever occur to you that *she* planned the whole thing?"

"I don't assume anything when it comes to you and Claudia," Emzee said. "But it's obvious that she's a better match for you. She always was!"

"I should probably go?" Andrew suddenly cut in, reminding both of us that he was still there. "I'll just let myself out."

"Good," I said, at the same time Emzee said, "no, don't go."

She looked at Andrew pleadingly.

"Sit back down," she insisted. "Please. I need you here."

She *needed* him? Was she being serious, or just trying to piss me off? The only person she needed right now was me —her fucking husband. Not this damn interloper.

"He doesn't need to be here for this," I argued.

Andrew was still standing in the threshold between the kitchen and the living room.

"Well I want him here," Emzee said stubbornly. "Andrew, stay."

"You can go," I told him.

Unsurprisingly, he didn't listen to me. Instead he walked past me and eased into a chair in the living room across from Emzee, who had plunked herself back down on the couch.

"This is a conversation between the two of us," I said. "Not the three of us."

"Do you think I want to be alone with you?" Emzee scoffed. "Maybe we should invite Claudia down here, just to keep things even."

"Claudia is *gone*," I said.

"How convenient. I hope you had fun together."

"*Nothing happened*," I said between clenched teeth.

141

"You always assume the worst when it comes to me and her, but we are done. We've been done for a long time, as I just reiterated to her before I threw her ass out of my apartment, Louis Vuitton luggage and all. She's out of my life for good!"

Emzee rolled her eyes.

"How could I not assume the worst?" she asked. "I came to your apartment and she was in your bed dressed in a fucking pink doily!"

"Jesus. She let *herself* in!"

"Which means she obviously has a key! Which you obviously gave her!" Emzee screamed. "Tell me again how I'm not supposed to be jumping to conclusions here, because usually when you give someone a key to your place it isn't because you want them out of your life for good!"

I scrubbed my hands over my face, almost laughing at how fucking ludicrous it all was.

"My *mother* gave her that key," I said as calmly as possible, praying Emzee would start to see the truth. "She planned this whole thing with Claudia behind my back. When I was in Chicago, she was nagging me nonstop for a key to the new place, and when I got home today I finally realized exactly why that was."

Emzee looked at me. I could see my words were finally beginning to sink in.

"You didn't give her that key?" she asked.

I moved toward her, and as I did, Andrew got up from his chair, but Emzee stopped him with an extended hand.

"Never," I told Emzee. "I swear to God. I wouldn't've given my mom a key at all if I'd known what she was going to do with it. And I'm going to call Louie as soon as I get back to my place and tell him I need to get the locks changed."

Emzee looked away and sighed, then met my gaze, her expression guarded and unreadable.

"Then...you really don't want Claudia?"

"Of course not. The only thing I want is *you*," I told her. "You and our kid and whatever kind of happily ever after we can make for ourselves. I'm here for all of it. The white picket fence, the smelly diapers, those embarrassing dog sweaters you get for Munchkin. I mean, if that's what you want, too. The decision is yours. You get to choose."

I heard a quiet intake of air from Andrew—guess he didn't know the happy news—but I didn't really care. Maybe it would finally convince him to back off.

"I love you," I added. If this was my last chance with Emzee, I didn't want to hold anything back. "I've always loved you. It just took me way too long to figure that out, but believe me when I say I'll happily spend the rest of our lives trying to make it up to you."

Emzee blinked up at me, searching my eyes, and then, as if we hadn't just been screaming our heads off at each other, gave me the kind of smile I had been waiting for since that night of the gala. "...I choose you, too."

I couldn't help myself. With one firm yank, Emzee was in my arms and her mouth was on mine, her hands clutching my shoulders as she melted into me. It was exactly what I wanted. Emzee in my arms. Everything felt right again.

Well, almost everything.

But as our tongues tangled, I heard the sound of her front door opening and closing. Thank God Andrew knew how to read a room and had shown himself out.

EMZEE

CHAPTER 21

I knew I was courting trouble by falling back into Ford's arms, but I couldn't resist. Not after he had completely poured his heart out to me during our fight. He *loved me*. Really, really loved me. He wanted to raise our baby, be a family, have a life together.

It could never actually happen, not with the deal I'd struck, but I let myself get carried away with the fantasy of it. It was impossible not to. Because regardless of the harsh, doomed reality of our situation, there was never any doubt: I'd always been in love with him.

Despite everything that had happened back in high school, the secrets and the lies, the fights, the breakups, none of it truly mattered in the grand scheme of things. In the end, I still loved Ford despite all the imperfections. Completely, unreservedly, and unshakably. And I was thrilled that he was the father of my child. He knew it, and he was excited about it, and I'd find a way to make him an equal part of the baby's life. In that regard, the Malones could kiss my ass.

"I love you," he murmured between kisses.

"I love you," I said back.

He swung me up into his arms, our mouths never parting. As he walked us toward my bedroom, I could hear Munchkin in the bathroom, scratching at the door and whining.

Pulling back, I said, "Sorry, he's freaking out. I need to—"

"Shh. I got it."

Once Ford laid me down on the bed, he went and let Munchkin out, then came back to the bedroom and closed the door. The tip-tap of tiny nails on the floor let me know that Munchkin was happy to retreat to his doggie bed in the living room.

I stretched out on the comforter, sighing happily as Ford climbed on top of me.

Oh, I had missed this. I'd missed the warm, reassuring weight of his body, the press of his hungry lips, the hard length of his cock digging against my thigh.

He stopped for a moment, his eyes focused on my face.

"I'm still really mad you didn't tell me about the baby."

Then he ripped my shirt off. I let out a squeal of outrage that was only half fake.

"I'm still mad your mother arranged a seduction," I told him as I tore at his belt and the button of his pants.

He groaned as I shoved my hands down his underwear, finding his cock and squeezing.

"Do NOT mention my mother when your hands are down my pants," he ordered.

"What are you gonna do about it?" I taunted, stroking him.

He gave me a wicked grin before I found myself flipped over onto my stomach, the rest of my clothes pulled off of me. I was facedown on the bed, completely naked, and I could feel Ford's heat through his clothes as he came up behind me, still fully dressed.

"Fuck, you look good," he said, slapping my ass hard enough to make me gasp. "And I already thought your ass was perfect."

"Shut up and fuck me," I commanded, laughing a little. "I won't be swayed by your sweet talk."

It made no sense, on the one hand, how easily we could go from fighting to fucking so quickly, but on the other hand, maybe it was simply an indication of how much passion we had for each other. The kind of passion I'd never had with anyone else I'd tried to date.

Ford shoved my legs open with a knee, his fingers finding my wet opening and slipping inside of me with ease.

"Mmm," I moaned, pushing back against him, riding his fingers. I knew it was only a preview of what was to come, but I was already hot and tingling with the friction.

I turned around to look at Ford and noticed the full-length mirror I'd propped against the closet doors. With a naughty grin, I said, "We need to face the other way. So I can watch."

He glanced over at the mirror and grunted with approval, immediately shifting our position so I could see myself on the bed on my hands and knees, my soft, full breasts hanging down, Ford on his knees behind me with his hand between my legs. We locked eyes in the reflection and I let my mouth fall open, moaning as I widened my stance, letting him finger me harder.

I'd watched porn before, but this was so much better. Seeing Ford's gaze go slack with lust, watching the way he was watching me, ogling him as he took off his shirt to reveal those tight abs, his perfect chest and broad shoulders. I arched my back so he could get a better view of my tits bouncing as I fucked his fingers even faster.

"Yes," I whimpered helplessly, feeling myself get closer and closer to the edge. "Yes."

"Let me see you come, baby," Ford growled. "That's it. Come for me. I want you to come right in my hand."

My eyes squeezed shut as a hard, hot orgasm slammed into me. I cried out, pressing my face into the blankets, trying to muffle my loud moans.

Before my body had even stopped shuddering, Ford was gripping my hips and pulling me back toward him. I could hear the clink of his belt buckle, the zipper of his pants.

"Give me that pussy," he said, teasing my entrance with the head of his cock.

"Yes," I moaned, my mouth watering. "It's yours. I'm yours."

"And I'm yours," he told me, squeezing my ass cheek before slapping it hard.

"Fuck! Again," I begged, watching him in the mirror.

He smacked my ass again, harder this time. I moaned at the sensation, the hot tingle under my skin, but before I could ask for another spanking, he thrust into me with a groan. We both cried out, my hands fisting the blankets as my body was suddenly jerked forward from the strength of his thrusts. Still watching our reflection, I pumped my hips back and forth, finding the rhythm, giving it to Ford as hard as I was getting it. His cock stretched me from the inside and I fucking loved it.

"You're mine," Ford grunted as he fucked me, eyes meeting mine in the mirror. "All mine."

I could feel his frustration and his anger in his thrusts, but as he fucked me, I could sense those feelings start to dissipate. His hands became more gentle on my hips, each

147

movement he made getting slower and deeper, like a promise of pleasure and more.

"Are you close?" he asked, leaning over me, his chest against my back, his voice hot in my ear.

Before I could answer, he moved his hand from my hip down to my clit, circling it with his finger. I cried out as he teased me gently, his cock and hand bringing me so much pleasure my eyes were watering. My second orgasm rose inside of me and I didn't try to fight it, moaning Ford's name as my release hit me in shockwaves. Ford kept fucking me, stroking my clit until it was all too much and I collapsed on the bed beneath him, feeling as if I'd been wrung out.

But he was still hard inside of me. It was clear that he wasn't ready for this to end.

I felt him withdraw, and then he turned me over and spread my legs wide, sliding back inside for more.

"Yeah," he groaned, positioning himself on top of me and clasping my hands, our fingers intertwined.

As he looked into my eyes, he began fucking me again, even slower this time, leaning down with each thrust to kiss me slow and deep.

"I'm sorry," he said. "I'm sorry about Claudia and my mother and everything."

I moaned, his dick so good and so right.

"I'm...sorry...too..." I told him. "I should have told you... about the baby. And I'm sorry about...the divorce papers."

I had to keep pausing to breathe and moan.

"I'm sorry about what I did in high school," he added. "I was an asshole. And I should have told you about your dad's...other business."

"I understand...why you didn't," I panted. "I...forgive you."

He stopped for a second, throbbing hot and hard inside

me, and for a moment I forgot what I was even talking about. All I could focus on was Ford and how good he felt.

"I love you, baby," Ford said, starting to pump into me again, picking up speed, grinding deeper and faster until tears came to my eyes.

"I love you too," I told him.

I'd been pushing back my feelings for so long that letting them out felt like a release—and it was immediately followed by a different kind of release. I came again, from some place deep inside, shuddering, gasping, my pussy clenching around Ford's cock and gushing wet as he thrust into me over and over again.

With a loud groan, he finally came too, spilling his release inside me, his hands still tight on mine. Rolling over afterward, he pulled me against his chest. Both of us breathing hard as we came back to reality.

I raised up on one elbow and looked at my husband. He turned his head to meet my gaze, that wolfish grin still on his lips—as if he'd never be able to get enough of me. Then he glanced down at my belly and that expression softened.

He reached out and put his palm over it.

"My baby's in there," he said, sounding awed.

"It is," I confirmed.

I knew that I owed him the explanation I'd been holding back. That coming *completely* clean with Ford was the only thing that would allow us to manage some kind of arrangement that would let him be a parent, while still keeping the senior Malones in the dark about the baby's true parentage. My brothers were keeping the Bratva's threats a secret from their wives, but I couldn't keep it from Ford. Not after everything we'd been through. I was done with lies.

At the same time, I also knew that once I told him the truth, he would be in danger as well. My stomach twisted as

I thought about what had happened just that afternoon at the bar. I didn't want to put anyone else in danger, but I also didn't want to keep hiding things from Ford.

If we were going to do this, we had to be on the same team. He had to know exactly what we were facing.

"Ford," I said. My tone was so serious, he immediately stopped stroking my belly.

"What is it?" he asked.

"I still can't really be with you," I said. "I'm sorry."

Immediately he sat up, his expression turning from peace and calm to anger and fire. We were probably destined to repeat our fuck-to-fight cycle unless I calmed him down quickly. I sat up too and put my hand over his open mouth.

"What I mean is, I can't be with you publicly," I clarified.

He relaxed a bit, but now the expression on his face was one of confusion.

"Let me explain," I said.

And then I told him.

I told him everything.

FORD

CHAPTER 22

After seven years of best friendship with Emzee, I had been under the impression that we basically told each other everything. Everything important, that was. School stuff, parent stuff, (her) bully stuff, (her) sibling stuff, dating and relationship drama, work and career shit, the occasional sex story. But as I sat and listened to her dump an overwhelming avalanche of information on me, I realized exactly how much she'd been keeping from me ever since we'd gotten fake-engaged. And what a burden it must have been on her to hold all those secrets in.

It all just poured out of her.

The Russian mob threats were somehow both completely shocking and also kind of unsurprising—a lot of dirty business had come to light during Emzee's dad's trial for sex trafficking, so I knew he'd had a connection to the Bratva, but I never considered that they'd turn around and put the heat on the Zoric children after Konstantin got put behind bars. It made sense, though. They'd lost a major stream of income when KZM's side hustle shut down, and they had the muscle and the guns to push Emzee and her brothers to keep handing over the money. Hearing about it from Emzee, it turned my stomach.

"They didn't care that the agency was going legit, that the trafficking was over, that things on our end had changed," she said. "They just wanted business to proceed as usual, with them getting a large cut of our profits. When they realized Stefan wasn't going to do that, they started making demands, to settle what they claimed were our 'debts.'"

She told me the number they'd demanded, and my jaw dropped.

"That is fucked. I'm so sorry," I told her. "What did your brothers do about it?"

She let out a sigh. "That's, umm, the other thing I have to tell you about. Stefan was only able to make a partial payment, and DRM can't take out another business loan, so...I had to figure out a way to pay off the rest. So the Bratva would leave us alone for good."

I felt the blood drain from my face. "You had to figure out a way...wait, what are you saying? Emzee, what did you do?"

Her voice dropped low. "I made a deal."

"A deal with whom? Why didn't you just go to the cops or the FBI or something?"

She shook her head. "I couldn't do that, Ford. Think about it. They'd never catch the guys who are after us, and even if they did, the Bratva would still be chasing us for the rest of our lives. If they didn't just hunt us down and make us disappear first."

My adrenaline was pumping. I couldn't imagine what kind of deal she'd made, but I hated the idea of it, of her getting involved in some shady underworld shit and putting her life—and our baby's life—at risk in the process. God knows what could have happened to her. Hell, it still could. This nightmare was long from over.

"So what's the deal?" I pushed. "Who's helping you?"

Looking at me, she tried to force a smile. She was clearly miserable. "Your parents."

"*What?*"

Suddenly, it all made sense. I'd known my parents had something on Emzee, since I'd overheard them pressuring her in their library before the See Yourself gala—but I'd assumed it was just minor dirt, the kind they thought was humiliating enough to blackmail her into walking out on me. The kind nobody would really care about. Which is why I'd barged in on them that night and declared my love, telling my parents I'd fight for Emzee and our relationship. I'd naively thought that making my intentions crystal clear regarding my wife would put an end to their meddling. That they'd back off.

I'd also thought that it would cement things between me and Emzee once and for good, but she'd walked out on me the very next day. Now I knew why.

God, my gut had told me she had real feelings for me right from the very beginning. So all the back and forth with her, the constant hot and cold, it was because of my parents and their "deal." I was glad to find out I hadn't been imagining Emzee's affections. But at the same time, the situation was so much worse than what I'd imagined. It wasn't just blackmail, wasn't just Emzee's reputation at stake—it was her life. Our *baby's* life. The lives of her entire family. This was the Russian mob, and they weren't the type to bluff when it came to threats.

I just couldn't believe my parents had known about the Bratva's extortion all this time and had used their power and money to strike this bullshit lose-lose deal with my wife.

Then again, of course they had. They'd been against my relationship with Em from the get-go, and I knew how much they wanted to control my life—my mother especially—there was no way they would have just stood by and let me be with Emzee without putting some sort of failsafe in place behind my back. Something to guarantee we wouldn't stay together.

"So they offered you money in exchange for a divorce," I said. "Enough money to pay off the mob. It was never about blackmailing you at all."

"They said they'd help me, but only if I agreed to leave you," she confirmed. "I'm sorry. It was the only way I could save my family."

I was seeing red, practically shaking with anger. I'd never felt so betrayed. And by my own fucking parents.

"So that night of the gala, when I walked in on you in the library—"

She nodded. "That was when they told me I couldn't get pregnant, or they'd let the mob go after my family. Your mom said they'd smear me in the press, deny the baby was yours.

"I didn't know I was pregnant yet, but the second I did, I knew they could never know the truth," Emzee continued. "Otherwise they'd never pay off the mob. So after the gala, I went to them and said that I'd divorce you right away. Before anyone could find out about the baby."

"I still don't get how they knew about your problems with the Bratva," I said. "Did you go to them for help?"

"No. They came to *me*," she said. "Right before the wedding. I don't know how they knew. I just assumed... maybe they had their own ties to the Russians somehow."

She looked up at me, her eyes worried and big. As if she was telling me something I hadn't already suspected.

As if I would be completely and totally shocked by this news.

"That makes sense. I've had access to my parents' lives for a long time. And I've seen plenty of things that made me think they had shady dealings. The first time being, you know, all those years ago—the day I heard them fighting about my dad sleeping with the models at KZM. Like I told you, that was how I found out about your dad and the trafficking stuff.

"I never really explained why I kept it from you. At first, I guess part of me wanted it to not be true. Like speaking it out loud would make it all real. By the time you and I became friends, I'd already buried it. Carrying those secrets around was a burden to me, and I cared too much about you to let it be a burden to you, too. I wanted to protect you."

"You did protect me," she pointed out.

"Not just from the bullies, but from everything ugly and harsh in the world. I know how shitty it is to find out your parents aren't who you thought they were," I said, letting out a sigh. "Who knows? Maybe my parents are the ones who introduced your father to them in the first place."

I pulled Emzee into my arms and leaned back against the pillows, rocking her a little, my mind on fire with all the bombshell revelations.

"I know I said this before, but I always loved you," I said. "Looking back, I think even when I couldn't see it, I wanted to protect you. Ever since I saw you hurting that first time, the hurt that I caused, I wanted to make things better for you. I wanted to make you happy."

Looking down at Emzee, I realized there were tears spilling from the corners of her eyes. As I wiped them gently with my thumb, kissing their tracks, she said, "What are we going to do, now that all our secrets are out?"

It was a fair question. We knew what we were up against—*who* we were up against. But that didn't mean the danger was gone. If anything, it seemed even more present, especially after learning that some fucking Bratva operative had tried to corner Emzee at the bar earlier.

I was not going to forgive my parents for this. They'd crossed a line a long time ago and it was time for me to push back. Emzee and the baby were my family now—not my parents—and I was going to make that perfectly clear to them.

But first, I had to figure out how to save my family.

"I'll take care of it," I promised her. "I'll find a way."

If we had to run away together, I'd do that, too.

I wasn't going to let anything come between us. Not ever again.

EMZEE

CHAPTER 23

Ford and I stayed up all night, holding each other and talking about the future. Making plans. Admitting our hopes and fears. That night turned into the rest of the weekend, which we spent ordering takeout, having sex, and trying to plan our next steps—and ultimately, what we were going to do about the Bratva and his parents and the money. Everything was fucked, on the one hand, but at least we were together now. We were a unit. A family.

We'd figure something out.

I was woken up just after five a.m. on Monday by my phone ringing. Ford groaned beside me in bed, and I fumbled for my cell on the nightstand.

"Hello?" I murmured groggily.

I was greeted by not one, but two familiar voices. My brothers. On a three-way call.

"Hey, Em," Luka said.

"Did we wake you?" Stefan asked.

My heart immediately started pounding. I quickly got

up and snuck out of the bedroom, not wanting to wake Ford, and settled on the couch in the living room.

"It's almost five in the morning," I pointed out. "Of course, you woke me."

"Sorry," Stefan said, but he didn't sound very sorry at all.

"It's urgent," Luka added.

Something bad must have happened. It was the only reason they'd be calling at this hour.

"What's wrong?" I asked, panic and morning sickness churning in my gut. "Don't try to sugarcoat it. Just tell me."

Munchkin came out of the bedroom, padding across the living room before hopping up on the couch next to me. Thank God for my dog. He always knew when I needed extra support.

"I had a...visitor tonight," Stefan said carefully. "From Russia."

My heart started pounding even harder. "Oh no. What happened?"

"Don't worry, he's gone now," Luka said. "Stefan had some words with him."

I pulled Munchkin into my lap, hugging him to my chest. "Oh shit."

"Yeah," Stefan said. "This is a hard line for me, and those fuckers have crossed it. Nobody messes with my family."

"Not that," I said. "I mean yes that, but...I have something else to tell you."

Quickly, I caught him up on what had happened to me at the bar, and how I'd sworn Luka to secrecy. It only served to piss off Stefan even more.

"I shouldn't have kept it from you," I told him. "I fucked

up. I hadn't even considered that the Bratva might send someone to put the heat on you, too."

"That asshole came to my house," Stefan said, his voice edged with fury.

I could hear the anger in his voice. My oldest brother was violently protective of Tori, and now that they had the baby, I would have been shocked if anyone from the Bratva made it back from a visit without some painful souvenirs of Stefan's displeasure.

"God, if anything had happened to you guys, I could never forgive myself. I'm so sorry," I said. I felt awful.

"Don't be. It's not your fault we're in this mess. It's fucking dad's fault," Stefan growled. "Bottom line is, protecting this family comes first, and I'll do whatever it takes to make sure they leave us all alone. For good. I couldn't live with myself if Tori or the baby became targets."

"Or Brooklyn and Little Kibbles," Luka added.

"*Little* Kibbles?" I asked. "Did you guys get another dog?"

"That's just what we call the baby to the dog," Luka said. "We've been telling him he's going to have a new brother or sister soon."

It was just ridiculous enough to make all of us chuckle a little. But I also realized that now was the time to tell my brothers about the secret I had been keeping from them. Because so much had changed, and with the Russians breathing down our necks, Stefan and Luka needed to know exactly what all of us were protecting.

I took a deep breath. I had so hoped that this moment would be completely different. That it would be like the happy moments my sisters-in-law had gotten, all champagne and excitement.

But there wasn't time for that now.

"Or...my pregnancy," I said. "I can't let anything happen to my little dude either."

There was a long silence.

"Emzee, are you saying..." Stefan began.

"Yes," I said. "I'm pregnant."

There was another silence.

"That's...great," Luka said hesitantly. "Holy shit, sis."

"Congratulations," Stefan added.

Their response was about as sober as I had expected. After all, we were essentially in a fight for our livelihoods and possibly our lives, and I had just announced something that could very much be seen as another liability. Even though I knew my brothers wouldn't think of the baby that way, I knew that they knew the Bratva would. And that was scary.

Luka echoed, "Yeah, congrats. I hope this is happy news?"

"It is," I assured him. "Ford and I are...talking. Just swear to me you won't tell your wives. I want to surprise them later. At least I can have *that* as an exciting reveal."

"Of course," Luka said.

"Sure," Stefan agreed. "As long as you promise not to tell them what's going on with the mob. I managed to make up some excuse when Tori asked why some Russian guy showed up at our door, but I don't want to risk her knowing more than she should."

"Same," Luka said. "Brooklyn does not need this kind of stress so late in her pregnancy."

It seemed to confirm that we were all on the same page as far as what we told the wives, which was nothing.

"I understand," I said, choosing not to mention that I'd already told Ford everything. "So what are we going to do?"

"I have an idea," Stefan said. "But I'm not sure either of you are going to like it."

"If it gets the fucking Russians off our back, I'll like it a lot," Luka said with passion.

"Same," I said.

Stefan let out a long breath. "Okay," he said. "Our obligation to the Bratva is reliant on them believing our business is still ripe for their use."

Already I could tell where he was going with this, and even though it made me a little sick, I also knew that it was probably going to be our best option. Especially since I no longer had the leverage I'd been counting on to get the Malones to pay off our debts. Once they found out that Ford and I weren't getting divorced, and that I was having his baby, the whole deal I'd tried to arrange would be off. This would be our only option.

We were going to have to take it.

Stefan continued, "If we can sell the business and give them the proceeds, it ought to clear us. They can find themselves another patsy. Because they won't keep coming to us if they know the well is dry. If there's no money or business in it for them, we aren't useful anymore."

There was a long silence as Luka and I absorbed what Stefan was saying.

"Okay. So we sell Danica Rose," Luka finally said. "I can't see another way out of this."

"Yeah. Agree," I said, pulling Munchkin closer. "But it still fucking sucks."

Stefan sighed heavily. "I know, but it's our chance to truly start over. Fuck, I might even recommend those assholes at Elite Image just for the pleasure of turning them in later."

Luka chuckled at that a little.

"But if we're really going to do this, we all have to agree that a sale is the only way forward. Even though it means no more family business," Stefan went on, and I could hear the disappointment and resignation in his voice. As the oldest brother, I was sure he felt like he'd somehow failed Luka and me by not being able to come up with some magical solution.

I felt the disappointment, too. Our father had built KZ Modeling, but after it had crumbled in the wake of the trafficking trial, my brothers and I had banded together and rebuilt the business from the ground up as Danica Rose Management, rebranding the agency and naming it after our late mother. It was the first big thing we'd ever really done as a family, and there was something utterly heartbreaking about knowing that our only option for a normal life, a safe life, was to give up something we'd all worked so hard to make happen.

"No more family business," I echoed in agreement.

"No more unlimited income," Luka said, but there was a dry humor to his words.

At that moment, I realized what else I would have to give up.

"No more non-profit," I murmured. The charity couldn't survive on donations alone. Danica Rose had been subsidizing the non-profit's cost of operations since day one.

"I'm sorry, Emzee," Stefan said. "I know how much See Yourself means to you."

"You've done amazing work," Luka added. "Helped so many people."

My eyes stung with tears. It was hard enough knowing I would have to give up my charity, take away life-changing resources from women who needed them, women who my father had hurt...but there was also something very poignant about my brothers acknowledging my efforts, and understanding how hard it would be for me to give it all up.

Letting go of See Yourself might end up being the worst decision I would ever have to make, but putting my family first was the one thing that my siblings and I all agreed on. The sacrifice we were making—putting our family before legacy, before money, before fame or reputation or business —was proof that we were a different kind of family than the one our father had tried to build. We were a different kind of Zoric than he had been. We always would be.

That knowledge made the sacrifice more bearable.

"Are we agreed?" Stefan asked.

The sun was just starting to come up outside my apartment window, rays of golden yellow and pale orange breaking through the clouds and making a dark silhouette of the Williamsburg Bridge. In so many ways, this was the start of a new chapter. Everything in my life had changed in the past few days. And it was going to keep on changing.

But for now, I knew the decision I had to make.

"Draw up the legal docs," I told my brothers. "And then courier them out to me so I can sign."

FORD

CHAPTER 24

When I left Emzee's apartment for the first time
—days later—it was only to get a change of
clothes from my place and charge my phone
back up. We had spent the entire weekend in bed, reuniting
and trying to plan our next steps. The last thing I wanted
was to face the real world again. Especially since I knew it
was a real world that wanted to drive us apart.

Not that it mattered. I was fully committed to Emzee
and our baby. I'd fight anyone who tried to separate me from
them again.

I also had to call Louie to ask about getting the locks on
my apartment changed, but my first priority was talking to
my parents. I was done dealing with their bullshit. They
had to back off my wife. As soon as my cell had juice, I'd be
making that call.

Not that I was ready to confront them about the depth
of their mafia ties yet. I was still trying to decide on the
best way to deal with that. Accusations would get me
nowhere, no matter how true they were. And I wasn't
naïve enough to think my parents would come right out

and admit what they'd done, apologize, and promise to break things off with the Bratva. If anything, they'd just pay lip service to me and then turn around and keep on doing what they'd always done. Or maybe it would create a rift between me and my parents that could never be mended.

Then again, maybe I was ready to cut myself off from the Malone family for good.

But that could wait. For now, I just needed to make it absolutely clear that I was with Emzee, now and forever. That I wouldn't tolerate any further attempts on their part to break us up. She was my wife, my *family*, and she was the most important thing in my life.

When I unlocked my apartment door, however, I realized that my plan to call my parents was entirely unnecessary.

Because they were sitting in my living room waiting for me.

"Ford! Where on Earth have you been?" my mother scolded, rushing over to me. "We were so worried. We've been trying to reach you for days, but you never picked up your phone."

She engulfed me in her embrace, overwhelming me with the cloying smell of her perfume and the rattle of all her jewelry. My father was still in a chair with the *Wall Street Journal*, per usual; he didn't bother to get up.

"What are you doing here?" I asked, stepping back from my mom and eyeing both of them suspiciously.

I highly doubted that either of them had actually been worried about me. But their visit reinforced the fact that I had to get a locksmith over, stat. It was bad enough that Claudia had shown up unannounced—but clearly she had reported back to good old Mom and Dad about her failure to seduce me, and now I had to deal with my parents' equally unwelcome surprise visit.

They obviously were not happy with whatever Claudia had told them.

So not happy, in fact, that they'd flown out to New York to talk to me in person. Actually, come to think of it, I was somewhat surprised (impressed, even?) that my father had skipped his standing weekday morning golf game for this.

"Claudia told us what happened," my mother said, breaking out her "disappointed" voice.

"Oh did she? So you heard all about how she broke into my apartment and got thrown out because she wasn't welcome here?" I asked.

"I gave her that key to check on you," my mother said, still trying to pout.

"I'm a grown man. I don't need to be checked on. Especially not by scantily clad ex-girlfriends," I said, adding, "I took her key back already. Now I'm taking yours."

"What?" Her eyes were wide. "Ford, I'm your mother. I need a key."

"Fine, keep it. I'm having the locks changed anyway."

My mother looked dismayed, but it did nothing to stop her from plowing forward with her coercion. "You need to apologize for the way you treated Claudia. She was very hurt."

"*She* was hurt?" I asked, holding back an incredulous laugh. "What about my wife and her feelings? Did Claudia happen to mention what she said to Emzee?"

"It hardly matters, Ford. You're getting a divorce," my mother said. "Regardless of what was or was not said, it's all water under the bridge."

I wanted to throw her under a bridge. "We're not getting divorced."

My father lowered his newspaper, frowning.

"Don't be ridiculous," he said. "You already signed the papers."

"I didn't. Emzee forged my signature," I said. "I'll fight it in court if I have to, and I'll win. Emzee and I are working things out."

My mother let out a little hiss.

"You *will* marry Claudia," my father said adamantly, tossing his paper on the table. "It isn't up for discussion."

"No," I said. "I won't."

"This is nonnegotiable," my father insisted, but I just shook my head.

"If you want her in the family so badly, why don't you marry her?" I said.

He narrowed his eyes and got up from the chair, pulling himself to his full height, which matched mine. He was seething. I couldn't remember the last time I'd seen him so furious.

"I'll cut you off," he said. "Your inheritance, all the money we have, you won't get a single penny of it. You'll be as good as dead to the family. And you think your job is safe at MREH? I was planning to have you take over when I retire, but you can say goodbye to that."

My mother sucked in a shocked breath. I wondered if she was thinking that my father had gone too far, but if she did, she immediately chose a side.

"That's right," she said, moving to stand next to my father in an attempt to present a united front. "You'll be entirely on your own."

It was obvious they thought they had me, judging by their smug expressions.

What they failed to realize was that I didn't care about the money, or my inheritance, or even my job at Malone

Real Estate Holdings. Hell, I could start my own real estate firm if I wanted to. I'd already been doing the lion's share of my father's job for years. Most of the employees would probably come with me. The only thing I cared about was Emzee and our baby. Our family.

Nothing else concerned me.

"I don't care," I told them. "It's not happening. I love Emzee. I'm staying with Emzee."

My father's face was turning red. He wasn't used to losing, but he had just played his only hand and come up empty. He didn't have anything else to use against me.

"You're being unreasonable," my father said.

"Me?" I asked. "I'm not the one trying to strong-arm their only son into some kind of arranged marriage."

"It's for your own good," my mother said.

I didn't believe that for a second. But me marrying Claudia had to be for someone's benefit—and I'd bet anything it was theirs. There was no other reason for them to be pushing me so hard.

"Why are you two so intent on getting me to marry her anyway?" I asked.

"Because she's the right choice for you," my mother said.

She couldn't have been further from the truth. In fact, the whole situation was so preposterous that I had to laugh. "No. You know what? I think it's because she's the right choice for *you*," I countered.

"She's the right choice for this family," my father clarified. "Because of the family she comes from. A family we've known for years."

"And what about Emzee's family?"

"They're dirty," my mother blurted out. "You *know* they're dirty. Everyone knows what Konstantin did with his business, and even if he's in jail now, his children are just like him. We can't be associated with those kinds of people."

"*Those kinds of people*," I said, nodding. Finally, hints of the truth were coming out. "Let me tell you about those kinds of people, Mom. They're honest, they're kind, and they run a tight ship over at the agency. Sure, KZ Modeling might have been dirty, but Danica Rose isn't. The fact is, you don't know anything about Emzee and her brothers."

"It doesn't matter what they're trying to do now," my father said. "That family has too many connections to the mob."

"And ours doesn't?" I asked.

"You can't speak to me that way!" my father said, his breathing shallow.

"You can't make me marry Claudia," I told him.

"You will marry her!" he said.

"Ford. Sweetie," my mother said gently, switching tactics. "We need you to do this. For us. Our entire family's reputation depends on it."

"That's right, son," Dad chimed in, trying to sound reasonable. "Claudia is clean. We need to appear clean, too."

I glared at both of them. "Of course you do. Because you *aren't*. Well, tough shit."

My mother let out a gasp.

"Watch your tone," my dad said.

But I wasn't hearing any of it. I turned to my dad. "I know the truth. You were involved with Konstantin years ago. You want to talk about dirty? You're just as dirty as he was."

"How *dare you*," Mom said.

They clearly weren't budging. Neither was I.

"It's not my job to be your PR," I told them. "This is

169

your mess, and me marrying Claudia isn't going to get you out of it. You have to figure it out yourself."

I didn't want to spend another minute arguing with them, having the same conversation over and over again that would get us absolutely nowhere. In fact, I didn't even want to be in the same room as my parents right now. They obviously cared more about their reputation and their money than they did for my happiness.

Turning my back on them, I went to my room to get a change of clothes, which I threw into a bag with my phone charger. Until I got the locks changed, I didn't plan on coming back.

"Where are you going?" my mother demanded as I passed them on my way out.

"To be with my family," I said over my shoulder. "The only family that matters."

From the expressions on their faces, I could tell that both of my parents were furious.

Walking out the door, I'd never felt so free.

FORD

CHAPTER 25

B ut all escapes from family—as everyone knows—are
temporary.

A mere week later, Emzee and I were headed
back to Chicago for her sister-in-law Brooklyn's baby
shower. As our flight descended into O'Hare, the familiar
layout of the city came into view below us: the Chicago
River, the dark monolith of the Willis Tower in the Loop,
the John Hancock Center overlooking Lake Michigan. The
sense that I was truly home again washed over me. It felt
nice.

Despite the fact that I was overjoyed to be back in the
city I loved and knew so well, however, I was also feeling
paranoid. I had no plans to see anyone from my old life
while I was in town, but all the same, it was anxiety-
inducing being on the outs with my parents. They'd gone
radio silent after our huge fight over Claudia at my
Williamsburg apartment, but they'd crossed too many
boundaries for me to be able to reach out and forgive them
just yet. And I was still infuriated by all the underhanded,

fucked-up things they'd done in order to keep me and Emzee apart.

Meanwhile, I didn't know what they were telling people about my absence from the city and the society events I usually attended with them. It was possible my reputation had already suffered some damage.

And then I reminded myself that I didn't care. That it wasn't my responsibility to back up whatever lies they were surely telling. It had given me a whole new appreciation for the grace that Emzee had always shown ever since people first started shitting on her back at Wayland-Blaine Academy. The guilt I felt over being the genesis of all that bullying might never leave me, but I felt like I was on a path to redemption at last. And it was a path I intended to stay on.

Speaking of bullies, Emzee hadn't been thrilled when I relayed the insults my mom and dad had hurled at the entire Zoric family, but I had reassured her that my parents' opinions had nothing to do with our future together. That their plot to coerce me into marrying Claudia had been futile.

I knew my parents loved me, in their way, and that in trying to protect themselves and their legacy they were also trying to protect me...but I had no room in my life for that kind of love and protection anymore. Emzee and the baby were all I needed.

At least I had been welcomed back into the Zoric family fold with open arms. I wasn't sure exactly what Emzee had told her brothers about our divorce, but I knew they were aware of her pregnancy, and the fact that she and I were back together for good.

The evening before the party, Emzee and I went over to Stefan and Tori's place for an early dinner and to visit the new addition to the family. Luka and Brooklyn were there, too.

"A baby changes everything," Stefan was whispering. "It really clarifies your priorities."

We were all staring down at the crib, where baby Nina was swaddled carefully in a circus animal print blanket. She looked drowsily up at all of us, half asleep and gurgling softly.

"She looks so peaceful," Emzee said.

"Oh, sure. She looks peaceful now, but she was up all night screaming her sweet little head off," Tori told us.

Both she and Stefan had dark circles under their eyes.

"I'm just trying to get as much sleep as I can before my little one comes," Brooklyn said, rubbing her round belly. "Zoric babies are loud when they don't get what they want." She winked at Luka. "Just like their fathers."

"You like it when I'm loud," Luka said with a grin. "Or was that the other way around—I like it when *you're* loud?"

"Oh, stop it," Brooklyn slapped his arm, grinning.

Stefan cleared his throat and looked at his watch.

"Aren't you ladies going to be late for your appointment?" he asked. He and Luka had arranged for the wives to get mani-pedis while the rest of us kept an eye on Baby Zoric.

"You're right, we'd better get going," Tori said.

We all tiptoed back out to the living room, and Brooklyn and Tori began gathering up their things. "Are you sure you won't join us, Em?"

Brooklyn clasped her hands over her chest. "Pretty please? We never get to see you anymore. I'm dying without our lunch dates."

"I wish I could," Emzee said. "But I'm not technically off the clock just yet."

"Oh, come on," Brooklyn wheedled. "You've been working so hard—look at the bags under your eyes. Your new boss is running you into the ground. You deserve a break."

It was true that Emzee looked tired, but for once, I couldn't blame Andrew for it. She hadn't been sleeping lately because of what was happening with the Bratva. That and her morning sickness. But she hadn't told her sisters-in-law about her pregnancy yet.

"I really need to get this project taken care of," Emzee said apologetically. "Plus, I don't want to miss a single second with Nina, especially now that I'm in New York all the time. You two enjoy. Let me take advantage of all the baby snuggles I can get while I'm still in town."

"I'm sure she'd love some quality time with Auntie Em," Tori agreed. "See you soon. We won't be long."

The minute she and Brooklyn were out the door, the conversation turned serious, the tone of the room shifting significantly.

"Okay," Luka said. "Time to get down to business."

Technically, Emzee hadn't been lying—she did have a project to take care of. Sending Tori and Brooklyn to the salon had been Stefan's way of getting the wives out of the house so that the Zoric siblings (and I) could have a family meeting about the situation with the Russians.

We sat around the dining room table, baby monitor propped up in the center so Stefan could keep an eye on Nina.

"These are the DRM board members we still need to convince," Stefan said, passing around a sheet of paper with a list of names on it. "They're not in favor of a sale, and we have to get them to come around without telling them too much."

"I'll get it done," Luka said, reviewing the list. "Leave it to me."

"Are there any other agencies you could offer to sell the company to, privately?" I asked. "Rather than outside investors who might not know how to run the business."

Emzee nodded. "Ford's got a point. I know you were joking about Elite, but we should keep all our options open. They were interested in buying us out before."

It was clear that Luka didn't like the idea of selling to Elite, judging by the expression on his face. "I'd hate to see them get their greedy hands on the business we built out of rubble."

"That's fair," Stefan said. "But at least they'd get all the strings attached to it as well."

They all shared a laugh, and then it got quiet again.

"Do you remember how we used to play tag in the hallways?" Stefan asked. "They're so long that it was the perfect length for games, even though it used to drive the employees up the wall having us running around like a bunch of wild animals."

"I kind of remember that," Emzee said with a wistful smile. "Or at least, I remember running after you. I could never catch you guys."

Luka grinned. "I remember. I always won, didn't I?"

Stefan cut in, "You wish! My legs were twice as long as yours."

"Pretty sure you cheated," Luka said. "You always cheated when we were kids."

"Me?" Stefan put a hand to his chest as if he was offended. "I'm not the one who'd break into the receptionist's desk to steal candy during her lunch break, even when she told us we were only allowed to have one piece. You always were the troublemaker."

"And you were always the one who told on me," Luka shot back. "I never would've gotten caught if you didn't tell her."

"What? She'd come back from lunch and catch you standing there with your hand in the drawer!" Stefan laughed. "And you'd swear the candy was for Em."

They reminisced some more, and I put my arm around Emzee, gently rubbing her shoulder to let her know I was there for her, even if I couldn't take part in the conversation.

I could see the look of longing on her face, the unconscious hand she'd placed on her belly. She didn't remember much about her mother, I knew that...but what she did remember was all tied up with the Danica Rose offices, the agency itself, and the paintings her mother had left behind when she died. Paintings the Zoric children had split up amongst themselves.

Stefan kept his on the walls all over the condo, so I was familiar with Mrs. Zoric's art. Modern, edgy, a little bit abstract and a little bit feminine, with hints of nude curvy bodies and glimpses of nature in the dark swaths of thick paint. I'd been told that Luka kept his canvases in storage, and I knew Emzee had hers boxed up at the loft, but she usually had one hanging in her bedroom. I think it hurt her to look at them too often. Or maybe it hurt her that she couldn't connect the art to her mother in the way she wanted to.

She'd described it to me as a hole in her heart, growing up without a mother. Her brothers had lost their mom at a young age, but at least they had memories of her, of being with her. Emzee had none. And yet it seemed like she'd projected all those years of yearning outward—it had manifested in the way she was so committed to caring for the women Konstantin had hurt. Helping them. Mothering them, in her own way. Providing for them what she herself had missed out on. That's what See Yourself was all about.

Which is why it was so fucked that my parents were forcing her hand. Forcing her to give up the non-profit, forcing all of the Zorics to give up their passions, their livelihood. It wasn't difficult to be on their side. As far as I was concerned, they were more family to me than the people who had raised me.

We all needed Danica Rose Management in different ways, but Emzee was the one who needed it most of all. The one who had done the most good with DRM's influence and scrubbed-clean reputation. I couldn't let this happen—couldn't just stand by while my parents manipulated my wife out of her last connection to her mother. Because the charity wouldn't be able to continue without DRM's financial support. Even if See Yourself was able to secure a ton of donations, it was Danica Rose's money that had been covering the salaries of the admins, the cost of the non-profit's rental space, the students' cameras, film equipment and photo developing supplies, and God knew what else. It'd take months, if not years, of fundraising to get the charity up and running again—and it'd always be on the verge of shutting down without outside support.

I had to say something.

"Listen," I said, pulling Stefan and Luka out of their memories. "We could all be unhappy, or just Emzee and I can be."

Stefan frowned. "I'm not sure you get a vote in this situation, but where are you going with this?"

"If Emzee and I go through with the divorce, my parents will cover your debts. The Bratva will walk away. You won't have to sell," I said.

"Em told us about the deal she made," Stefan said. "And

while I appreciate the sacrifice you both are willing to make, I can't in good conscience support it. We're not going to break up your marriage just to save the agency."

"Agreed," Luka said. "Family first."

"I understand that. But I think you need the agency," I said. "All of you."

"With all due respect," Luka said, with an edge to his voice, "I don't think you know what we need."

"We have to sell the business, Ford," Emzee said gently. "It's the only way."

Stefan started to join in with their protests, but I shook my head.

"Can you not hear yourselves?" I waved my hand at the table. "Because I just listened to a hell of a lot of compelling reasons for you to keep DRM. You spent the last ten minutes talking about your great memories growing up in that building—growing with the business. It's clear the company was responsible for shaping all of you into the adults you are. It's your *legacy*."

I watched as the brothers exchanged a look. It was hard to tell if they were going to tell me to shut the fuck up or if they were finally considering what I was saying.

As for Emzee...her face was schooled into the kind of neutral blankness that I now knew was just a cover for heartbreak. Of course she wanted to keep the company in the family. She was faced with an impossible decision. Lose me, or lose DRM.

Suddenly the baby monitor squawked, and we could hear the baby start to cry.

Stefan rose, but Emzee was on her feet faster, waving her brother away.

"I'll go rock her," she said. "I could use the practice."

I followed her, standing in the doorway of the baby's

room as she turned on the light and reached into the crib to take Nina out. Cradling the baby, she crossed the room to settle in the rocking chair by the window. Nina quieted almost immediately, staring up at Emzee with her big, round eyes. As I watched the two of them rocking slowly together, I could almost see our future. The way Em would be holding our child soon.

But first, we had a lot to sort out.

"I can't change the past," I told her. "I'm not even sure I can change the future. My parents are always going to be assholes. But here's what I want for *your* future, Em."

She didn't look up, her eyes fixated on the baby, but I knew she was listening.

"It's taken me a while, but I've come to realize how important the non-profit is—how much value your work with those women has, for them and for you. I've seen how you interact with them, how you lift them up. How you strive to make their lives better. And I know just from watching you that you're going to be an amazing mother to our child.

"But I also know that our child getting the chance to grow up playing tag with their cousins in the hallways of Danica Rose, and watching Mommy save the world, is the best thing I can offer."

Emzee finally looked up at me, tears in her eyes. Realizing the same thing that I already had: we were going to have to break up. Once and for all.

"I know it'll be hard," I told her. "We can't ever say the baby is mine. But I want you both safe, more than anything, and this is the only way we can make that happen."

My eyes were starting to sting, too, but we had no other choice. Going along with my parents' deal felt like the best plan. And it would save Danica Rose. Save the Zoric legacy.

Secretly, though, I had a Hail Mary in my back pocket. And even though Emzee and I had promised not to keep secrets anymore, I knew that I had to keep this from her.

Because if it exploded, she couldn't be anywhere near the devastation.

EMZEE

CHAPTER 26

No matter what I said to Ford or how hard I tried to convince him that we could find a way to be together, I may as well have been trying to reason with a brick wall. Ford had made up his mind. In order to make his parents happy, we had to be apart.

So here I was now at Brooklyn's baby shower, depressed and alone.

It was being held at her and Luka's apartment, and since Brooklyn was literally a fashion model, it was decorated like no other baby shower I'd ever been to.

Instead of soft pink and blue pastels, my sister-in-law had chosen the Pantone colors of the year—a deep, bright yellow and a cool gray—for her theme colors. There were also splashes of gold everywhere, because nothing said Brooklyn like glitter and glam. Gold stars and moons made of paper hung from the ceiling, along with three-dimensional old-timey hot air balloons instead of regular balloons. Cream and yellow flowers practically exploded from every surface.

Meanwhile, Luka was making the rounds with trays of

bite-sized appetizers and drinks. I got a kiss on the cheek and a plate of mini souffles from my brother, but he was too busy being a good host to hang out and commiserate with me.

I'd just reached up to touch one of the hot air balloons when Tori came up beside me with Nina in her arms.

"Aren't those so cute?" she said. "I found them on Pinterest. They're handmade and they came all the way from France."

"How gratuitous," I whispered, as if I was scandalized by the thought. "I love them."

"Me too," Tori said. "I already called dibs on the pink one for Nina's room."

"I'm so glad you're here. And how is my sweet angel?" I cooed, reaching down to gently trace the baby's hairline with my finger. "Hi, sweet girl. Just look at all those dark curls."

Nina smiled at me, and maybe it was just gas, but I didn't care. She was beautiful.

"Want to take her for a minute?" Tori asked. "I have to run to the ladies'. We got caught in traffic on the way over and I've been holding it. Stefan's still bringing the presents up."

She passed Nina into my arms and I found a quiet corner to hide in at the end of the hall. I knew Tori would be bombarded by guests with their own cases of baby fever for most of the party, so I was happy to have a few minutes with my niece all to myself.

When Tori found us, I was rocking Nina in my arms, my lips pressed to her forehead.

"You're a natural," Tori whispered. "I brought you a champagne flute so we could trade."

I laughed. "Thanks."

Once we returned to the party, I discretely tipped the champagne into a potted plant and grabbed a bottle of water instead. I still hadn't shared my big secret with my sisters-in-law yet.

The agenda was packed full of party games and gift opening and generally being elbow-to-elbow with people I didn't know. Between the loudly chattering guests and my usual nausea, I couldn't force myself to sit with the group for too long, so I settled into a chair at the edge of the room and picked at a cupcake while Brooklyn's best friend Mateo set up the games.

The first involved trying to put cloth diapers on balloons with safety pins, which resulted in many popped balloons, a lot of laughing, and one spilled drink (not mine).

Up next was a trivia game about Brooklyn and Luka, where we were given a list of traits and we had to guess who they described. I knew Brooklyn was crazy about chocolate-covered strawberries and that Luka was the better ice skater (thanks to his many years on the boys' hockey team), but I still lost the game, too distracted by my thoughts to finish filling in the blanks. I missed Ford.

After that, we sat around decorating diapers for Brooklyn and Luka to use during late night changings. We were supposed to write words of encouragement, draw pictures, sign our names. I sketched Mr. Kibbles, Luka and Brooklyn's greyhound, and drew a little speech bubble coming out of his snout that said, "CHANGE IS RUFF!"

The dog part looked pretty good, but I'd never said I was a comedian.

All the while, women were circling Tori and Nina and talking about what a pretty baby she was, how tiny, how perfect, how precious. Telling stories about their own babies, their own pregnancies, their remedies for colic and teething and overall reassuring Brooklyn that she was going to do great during the delivery, that everything was going to be completely wonderful.

On the outside, I was smiling. Inside, it felt like there was a knife in my chest.

Of course I wanted to be happy and excited for Brooklyn, but being at her shower was just a painful reminder of all the things I wouldn't be getting when I eventually told people about my surprise New York baby. The baby that everyone would "know" was the result of an affair.

The Malones wouldn't have to spread a word of that rumor, either, because everyone could do the math. Thanks to all of Ford's foot-dragging on signing the divorce papers, I'd run out of time to pretend that we'd gotten divorced first and I'd gone to a sperm bank afterward. Now it would just look like he'd found out I was cheating and we'd separated because of it.

Not that I could blame him for refusing to sign. His heart had been in the right place.

But even so...just thinking about what could have been still hurt.

Thankfully, Luka was done passing out cocktail weenies and Stefan was leaning against a wall with a whiskey in his hand, so I wasn't completely on my own. In fact, my brothers looked almost as out of place as I felt. Most of the guests were Brooklyn's friends, so it was a lot of screaming women helping her open gifts and taking pictures of everything she unwrapped.

"This almost makes me not want to have kids," Luka said, coming to stand by me with a freshly opened beer.

"No, it doesn't," Stefan said.

Luka grinned at his extremely pregnant wife who was sitting on her baby shower throne looking gorgeous and glowing. I was pretty sure that when I started showing, I wasn't going to look anything like Brooklyn and Tori had. I was too short and too curvy already—a baby would just make me look like a beach ball with legs.

"Sorry you have to be here without Ford," Stefan said, putting his hand on my shoulder.

"Sorry for all of it," Luka added quietly.

They were trying to console me on the sly, since their wives still didn't know anything about the Bratva, or how seriously close we had come to losing the family business... or what the cost had been for me personally. But although I truly appreciated their efforts, there wasn't anything my brothers could say that would help, that could change the fact of my impending divorce or make the situation any better.

I was always going to be playing this role in our family. The martyr. The one who got the crumbs while they feasted. It was like I was goddamn Munchkin: a little dog, always curled up at their feet, waiting for attention. I wished that Munch was with me now. He wasn't a substitute for Ford, but he had always been a great comfort to me.

"What are you three scheming about?" Tori teased, walking over to us with the baby in her arms.

"Work stuff," Stefan said, kissing his wife and then Nina. "Nothing important."

"I'll bet," Tori said with a smile.

All of a sudden the lights in the room dimmed, and everyone stopped talking. I turned in my chair to see Tori's stepmother Michelle walking slowly into the room, carrying a white frosted cake decorated with gold leaf and real peonies, ablaze with candles. It was beautiful. The smell of vanilla and flower petals had my mouth watering already.

"A birthday cake? What is this?" Brooklyn asked, looking delighted.

"Birthday wishes can be made in advance," Tori's step-mother said with a smile. "So let's all wish good things for Brooklyn and Luka's little one."

She placed the cake in front of Brooklyn, the lights from the candle making her look even more luminous. Luka went to her side, and took her hand in his. As everyone sang "Happy Birthday," my brother and his wife smiled at each other with such love that my heart almost burst. At the end, while everyone was applauding, they blew out the candles together.

The whole thing was extremely adorable, and it reminded me that even as I was stewing in my jealousy and loneliness, at least I *had* a family. No matter what happened —with my marriage, with the mob, with the agency, with the baby's perceived paternity—I knew that I had two brothers who were fiercely protective, and two sisters who were the kind of friends I'd only ever dreamed of while I was growing up.

Ford, on the other hand, didn't have anything like that. He had no one to swap memories with. No one to share the good times with. No one who had his back no matter what. Except...me.

I wished that I could have saved Ford the way he had saved me all those times before. The way he had protected me and taken care of me.

Then I realized something. I could.

FORD

CHAPTER 27

I was sleeping when I heard the key turn in the lock. My suitcase was on the floor, packed and ready for my flight back to New York the next day. My first thought when I heard someone come through the door was that my parents—or Claudia—were up to more of the same old tricks.

But as I padded down the hall in my boxers, ready to kick out whoever had dared to sneak into my apartment, I saw a familiar silhouette standing in the entryway.

"Emzee?"

Thank God I hadn't already gone back to New York yet to clean out my apartment in Williamsburg. My heart ached to see her, but I was also wary. We'd agreed that for all intents and purposes, we would be over. It was the only way to get my parents to cooperate and pay off the Zorics' debt to the Russians. Emzee being at my place could put all of that in jeopardy.

"You can't be here," I told her softly.

She ignored me, and I followed her back to my room, where she unzipped her dress, letting it slide to the floor. I

187

couldn't help it, I was already hard for her. It had only been a day, but I wanted her desperately.

"We have to be over," I protested weakly as she took off the rest of her clothes.

Then she climbed into bed, naked and waiting.

God, she was gorgeous. I wanted to touch her more than I wanted my next breath. It took all my willpower to hold myself back.

"Em, this is a bad idea," I said.

"Where are the new divorce papers?" she asked.

I'd had a new set of them drawn up by my lawyers and had planned to send them to Emzee for signing once we were both back in New York.

"In my suitcase..." I gestured at the packed bag on the floor, but I was confused about what she was getting at. "Why?"

"Get them for me."

I was in no rush to have her sign them now, but if that's what she wanted, I knew I would have to do it. Feeling resigned, I went to my suitcase and dug out the papers that were tucked inside a manila envelope with her address already written on the front. Then I walked over to the bed and handed the papers to her, expecting her to grab the pen off of my bedside table and sign them right there.

Instead, she flipped through the pages one by one, sighing as she skimmed the legalese.

"What's wrong?" I asked. "Do you need me to change something?"

Looking up at me, she smiled. "I don't need you to change a damn thing."

Then she held up the papers and ripped them in half. And in half again. Soon, the floor was covered in divorce document confetti.

I was shocked. It was the last thing I had expected her to do. "What was that for?"

"We don't need it anymore."

Sighing, I sat down on the bed beside her. "Em, I told you, I'm not letting you sell the agency."

She shook her head.

"That's not the plan," she said. "I have my own plan now. I'm going to fix all of this. You just have to trust me."

"I do trust you." But at the same time, I was dubious.

On the other hand, I'd been a wreck without her, and we'd only been apart for one day.

"I trust you," I repeated, "but I need to know what your plan is. Because I have some ideas, too."

"We can talk later," she said, wrapping her arms around my neck and pulling me on top of her. "First, I want you to make love to me."

I didn't need her to ask twice. With her in my arms, there was no way I could have resisted. Not that I wanted to.

I kissed her roughly, so hungry for her I could barely control myself. She returned my kiss with the same intensity, her fingers sliding all the way down my back to squeeze my ass, holding tight as she started grinding against me. Her pussy was so wet, I could feel it through the fabric of my boxers.

"Fuck," I groaned, lifting my hips so she could pull off my underwear.

We were both naked now. My cock was hard enough to slip right into her, but I held back. I wanted to go slow, savor every last drop of her.

Our tongues stroked against each other as I gripped her hair in my hands. We were kissing as if we'd been separated for days, months, years, and I couldn't get enough of her taste—that sweetness that was pure Emzee. I could have kissed her forever. I was drunk on her. On the way I felt when I was with her, and especially when I was inside of her.

Rolling over so that she was on top, I ran my hands up the back of her thighs, skimming the curves of her ass before wrapping my arms around her. All I wanted was to hold her close and never let her go. Our kisses slowed, becoming softer and more gentle.

As she moaned quietly, I thought back on all the lies and secrets we'd kept from each other over the years. How they had almost destroyed us. Now, there was nothing between us. We were completely naked to each other, figuratively and literally.

I shifted Emzee higher, so her breasts were level with my mouth, and then wrapped my lips around her nipple. Then I sucked. Softly at first, then harder. She gasped, threading her fingers through my hair, pulling me even more firmly against her. I licked and circled and sucked some more, then switched to the other one, my hand coming up to play with the peak I had just teased with my mouth.

Emzee's hips were grinding against mine, her pussy wet and ready against my shaft, but I kept holding back. She'd asked me to make love to her, and that meant pacing myself.

"Ford," she moaned. "That feels so good."

Her cries of pleasure made me even harder, my balls aching, but I didn't want to rush. Instead, I kept up with the foreplay, taking my time with her breasts and letting her grind against me until she came. Not the kind of earth-shattering orgasm she usually had, but a small taste of what was in store for her. Still, it left her gasping.

"Lean back," I told her, pushing her gently off me.

Even in the dark, I could see that her skin was still

flushed and her eyes were barely focused. I wanted to take her over the edge again. Make her beg and moan and scream my name. I wanted to finger her tight, perfect pussy, taste her on my tongue as I fucked her with my mouth, feel her walls clench hard around my cock as she came with me plunging deep inside of her.

I wanted all of her.

"I love you, Em."

She looked up at me, her luscious mouth parted. "I love you."

I slid down, pressing my mouth to her stomach, leaving kisses on her belly where I knew the baby was growing.

Then I moved lower, trailing soft kisses across her hips as my fingers traced her wet slit. She was ready for round two, I could feel it, but I took my time. First, I touched her with my tongue, one long lap from her ass to her clit, making her moan. Her legs were spread wide and I made a place for myself between her thighs, licking and sucking every part of her pussy until my jaw started to ache. She tasted so good I wanted to lap her up, every last drop, wanted to lose myself in her sweet taste and her scent.

I groaned as I ate her out, letting her know how much I loved it, how turned on I was. Her hands were in my hair, pulling harder as I sucked her whole clit into my mouth again. I knew exactly what she liked, exactly what got her off, and I loved how responsive she was to me.

"Fuck," she panted. "I'm going to come again."

I tightened my grip on her hips, spreading her legs even wider as I stroked her with my tongue. She wouldn't be able to hold out much longer, judging by the way her breath was coming faster and faster, her grip on me growing even firmer. She was moaning my name as I licked her harder, fucked her with thrusts of my tongue, my fingers, the sound of her like music to my ears, not stopping until she cried out at last with the pleasure of her release.

That was it. I was done being gentle. I didn't even wait for her to stop shuddering before I was spreading her lips and inserting my fingers. One, then two, and then three. I wanted to stretch her, to prepare her for my cock. She took each finger with a groan, begging for more, her hands moving to the bed to clutch the sheets as I fucked her hard with my fingers.

My thumb found her clit, which I knew had to be sensitive still, but I rubbed it hard, knowing that I could make her come one more time before I plunged my cock deep inside her.

"Come on my fingers," I commanded. "I own that pussy. It's mine. It belongs to me."

"Yes," she gasped. "It's yours."

Sweat had broken out along my brow, but I knew I had to control myself just a little longer. I wanted to give her as much pleasure as she could stand. It was only after she climaxed a third time, yelling my name so loud I was certain she would wake the neighbors, that I finally rose onto my knees and positioned myself between her legs.

Sliding into her was the sweetest sensation I'd ever felt. I began fucking her hard and fast immediately, the hot, wet tightness of her pussy almost too much to bear. She felt so good, so right, and I knew by the way she was wrapping her arms around my neck and her legs around my hips that she felt just as good as I did.

"Nothing will ever separate us again," I told her. "I promise."

"Promise," she repeated, biting her lip as her eyes closed.

I was thrusting fast, breathing faster, needing to be even

deeper inside her. I pushed her legs up higher around my waist and felt my cock inch more fully inside of her. It felt like heaven. Emzee let out a low moan, her fingers digging into my biceps.

"Yeah, oh God, yeah," she was saying, over and over.

"Yes," I moaned.

Holding her hips steady, I began fucking her harder, wanting to make her come one more time before I spilled my seed into her sweet, wet pussy. Her lush tits were bouncing with each thrust, her mouth open, her eyes closed. It was the most beautiful sight I'd ever seen. My hands were everywhere, cupping a breast, squeezing her ass, gripping her hip. I couldn't get enough.

"Ford. Yes. *Yes.* Come with me."

"I am. And I'm never letting you go," I told her, feeling myself start to lose control. "You're mine. You're mine forever."

"Yes," she cried out. "Come inside me."

It was enough to trigger my own release. Groaning, I spilled deep inside her, feeling her pussy clench around me with every hot spurt. Her head went back, her moans pitching higher as I fucked her through her orgasm. I didn't even lose my rhythm—it was like my dick had been hard for so long, it just couldn't stop.

Once the aftershocks stopped, I lay there, my head against her breasts. Her arms were wrapped tight around me, our bodies slick with sweat. As I drifted off to the sound of her heartbeat, rhythmic and steady, I knew that whatever we had to face, we would face it together.

EMZEE

CHAPTER 28

My hands were shaking with nerves. The whole car ride over, Ford had held them firmly in his lap and that had made me feel better, but now, standing in the entryway of the Malones' brownstone, knowing we were about to face his parents, I couldn't stop them from trembling again.

Ford and I had agreed on a plan, but I had no idea if it was going to work. We'd promised that we were in this together, but I was afraid of what would happen if we failed. I was afraid what would happen to my brothers and sisters-in-law, to my niece and Brooklyn's baby. What would happen to my own tiny, new family. My husband. My baby.

But I also knew that I was done letting the Malones make all the decisions for us. I knew that we had to fight back, even if it scared me to death.

At least Ford was at my side.

He linked his fingers with mine and we headed to the dining room. His parents were expecting him for dinner, alone—so I had a feeling they were going to throw a fit the moment they saw me with him.

I wasn't wrong.

We walked into the room, and Mama Malone was up and out of her chair within seconds. Father Malone even deigned to put his newspaper down.

"What is she doing here?" Ford's mother sputtered.

She was speaking to Ford, but I was the one who answered.

"I have an announcement," I told them. "One you'll want to hear."

"Well." Ford's dad sighed, and he got up, too. "I imagine we'll have more privacy in the library."

"Dad—" Ford started.

"Suits me," I said brightly. "Shall we?"

Honestly, I wasn't interested in spending an entire meal—or any portion of one—with Ford's parents. And besides, Ford and I planned to leave as soon as this was through.

Once we were all seated, with the exception of Ford, who stood beside my chair, Mrs. Malone huffed, "Well? What the hell is going on?"

A bit smugly, I announced, "I have an ultimatum for you. Both of you."

Ford's parents sat back, clearly annoyed.

"Here's the deal," I went on. "You can get my family out of trouble with the mob, or I can do it myself. Either way, Ford and I are staying together."

I reached over and took my husband's hand. "That's nonnegotiable," Ford added.

Mrs. Malone was speechless, for once. They both looked incredulous that I had the nerve to show up at their house and make demands. Ford's father was the first to respond.

"Why would we help you out if you stay with Ford?" he

asked, clearly confused. "You know that was the price of our assistance. No divorce, no assistance."

I was nervous, but I lifted my chin, trying to be brave.

"Because if you don't help us out, then you'll be even further connected to the mob. Because I'll have to give my shares of the modeling business to the Russians. It will replace the money they want from us, but it will also permanently tie them to my family."

"How is that *our* problem?" Mrs. Malone asked sourly.

"Because as long as I'm with Ford—"

"Which will be forever," he interrupted, fixing his parents with a stare.

"—then that means your family is tied to mine," I finished.

I let those words sink in before I continued, the senior Malones eyeing each other uncomfortably. They were smart people—manipulative and sly, yes, but clever—and I was pretty sure they were connecting the dots on their own, but I was going to make sure they knew exactly what would happen if they didn't agree to our terms.

"Right now the Zoric family and Danica Rose Management have very shiny PR. If someone finds out, years from now, that these payments to the mob have been happening, it will look like business as usual—that is, the kind of business that my father ran under the KZ Modeling name—was still going on."

I fixed my stare at Father Malone.

"And everyone will assume that you knew all along."

The plan wasn't ideal—my family *had* gone clean and I didn't want to force them into a partnership with the mob— but I was counting on the Malones to have a change of heart after they heard us out.

"There's more," Ford added.

His father gave him a look that could have peeled wallpaper. I smiled sweetly.

Ford had told me that morning about his Hail Mary. Because now that we'd figured out a way to be together no matter what, he'd felt his backup plan was something he could share.

The Malones were going to be furious once they heard it.

"I've been collecting information on you," Ford continued. "The documentation I have is somewhat sketchy, but it's enough proof to turn you in."

I saw the color in Ford's father's face drain away. Mrs. Malone was clutching the arms of the chair she was sitting in as if she was afraid to let go.

"It'll never hold up in court," she said, but her voice was squeaky with panic. Obviously, she understood the trouble they were in. I wasn't sure Ford's father, with the stubborn set of his jaw, was thinking as clearly as she was.

Ford shrugged. "It doesn't have to. At the very least, I could leak enough to make things look very scandalous. Enough to ruin your reputations for good."

That seemed to snap his father out of his daze. "You turn us in, you're only hurting yourself," he said, drawing himself up straighter in his chair. "This whole empire I've built would be destroyed. All your inheritance, gone."

"Doesn't matter to me," Ford said. "I've built my own empire, completely separate from yours."

He was proud of that, and he should have been. He'd worked hard to separate himself from his family name and he would be fine if he had to walk away from MREH for good. He had all the contacts and connections he'd need to start his own business. Maybe even in New York.

That realization was clearly a blow to the Malones, but we weren't done with them yet.

"There's still one more thing," I said.

Mrs. Malone shot daggers at me with her eyes. But they barely landed, glancing off of me instead. I'd gotten stronger in the time I'd been with Ford. Her disapproval couldn't touch me.

"If you decide not to help us out," I continued, "then we'll remain close enough to you to keep the mob ties a concern, but you will have absolutely nothing to do with our child."

I put my hand over my belly, and Ford squeezed my shoulder.

"You're pregnant?" Ford's mother asked, her voice barely a whisper.

I held my breath, afraid I might have counted too much on Ford's parents caring about his offspring. It had been a gamble to think they would prioritize a grandchild over their money and reputation, especially since it had become clear that they didn't prioritize Ford in that way.

"Yes," I confirmed. "And yes, it is Ford's."

Mrs. Malone turned to her husband.

"We can't cut off our only grandchild," she said.

I felt Ford relax next to me, and I squeezed his hand, relieved beyond measure.

Ford's father looked less convinced, but as usual, he also didn't look like he was going to argue with his wife. The senior Malones had some kind of silent conversation with their eyes, and then Mr. Malone turned his attention back on me and Ford.

"The Russians won't be a problem for you anymore," he said.

∼

THE MINUTE FORD and I were in a car heading home, we both let out a whoop of joy. Then he took me in his arms and kissed me until I could barely see straight.

"I wish I could have a glass of champagne," I told him, even though I was feeling giddy enough that I didn't really need alcohol. "We should celebrate."

"Oh, we will," Ford said with a smirk. "But the kind of celebrating I have in mind doesn't require champagne."

I blushed, knowing that the minute we got home, we would be in each other's arms again.

And this would be our life together from now on. We didn't have to pretend, we didn't have to hide, we didn't have to keep secrets.

We leaned back against the seats, lost for a moment in our own little world, Ford's arm around my shoulder, both of our hands against my stomach.

"Do you think the baby is what changed their mind?" I asked.

"Maybe. I think they realized they were fucked and the baby just gave them a reason to do the right thing. As much as they *can* do the right thing."

"Do you think they'll want to be in the baby's life?"

The thought of possibly having to attend weekly dinners with Ford's parents was one I didn't like considering.

"We won't be spending much time with them, especially if we decide to stay in New York," Ford promised. "But from now on, *we* get to decide how much we want them in our lives. Or in our baby's life."

"I like that," I said.

"And the important thing is, you didn't have to sell the business."

"Yeah." I smiled. "Danica Rose gets to stay in the family. Exactly where it belongs."

I relaxed even further into his arms, feeling a sense of relief that I hadn't felt in months—that I hadn't felt since Stefan first told me that the Bratva was after us.

"And," I added, "I didn't have to bring the mob back into my brothers' lives."

"Feels nice, doesn't it?" Ford asked, pulling me closer.

"So nice," I said, letting out a sigh.

It was true that we would always have the shadow of a connection to the underground through Ford's parents, but it was worth it in the end.

Because we were finally free.

This was a whole new beginning for us, and I could hardly wait.

EPILOGUE

EMZEE

I barely got a glimpse of the room before Tori threw herself into my arms and gave me a huge hug. All I saw were balloons. Tons and tons of balloons. In all my favorite colors: deep purples and burgundies, rich teal, sleek black and silver. I was sure Brooklyn had picked them out. She'd never been one to go for classic pink and blue.

"I am so excited to meet your baaaaaaaabbbb-byyyyyyyy!" Tori squealed, wrapping her arms around me and forcing me to jump up and down with her.

I didn't mind. After all, her happiness was infectious, and it was clear that she and Brooklyn had put a ton of work and love into planning this shower. Once I extracted myself from Tori's grip, I got a chance to look around and see what my sister-in-laws had done.

"This place looks amazing," I exclaimed.

The room was full of balloons, but it was also decorated with streamers and ribbons and almost every surface was covered in beautifully wrapped gifts. I was surrounded by love and excitement.

I couldn't have asked for a better baby shower.

Well—baby sprinkle, supposedly. At least, that's what my sisters-in-law had promised, but I'd known the moment I asked for something small that they wouldn't be able to resist going all out, and I'd caught the look that passed between them when I said I didn't need a full-blown extravaganza.

Still, by the third baby you'd think they might have a little more chill...though I was secretly glad they had ignored my wishes. It was a nice reminder of how much they cared.

"I told you they'd never let you get away with a small shower," Ford whispered in my ear as he came up behind me.

He wrapped his arms around my growing belly and I leaned back into him with a contented sigh. I would have thought that after two kids, and with a third on the way, that the sparks between us might have dulled a little. But Ford always insisted that I was never sexier than when I was pregnant. Which is probably why we were having a third. He could barely keep his hands off me when we weren't expecting, but when I was, it made him almost ravenous.

From the look in his eyes now, I could tell that he was debating dragging me off to the guest bedroom to push me up against a wall and have his wicked way with me. If we weren't surrounded by family and friends—all of whom had worked so hard to make this shower possible—I might have let him.

Instead, I just tilted my head back for a kiss and then watched all the oldest kiddos (Nina, Dani, and Teo) playing tag down the long hallway outside the apartment. Our middle child Rosie was sitting in a playpen with Tori and Stefan's youngest, Milan, the two of them laughing hysterically at some game of swapping toys that only they seemed to understand, despite the fact that neither of them could speak in complete sentences yet.

It had been five years since Ford and I had made our last stand against his parents, taking a risk on our future and our happiness. A risk that had since paid off, with dividends. Life was truly grand.

True to their word, the Malones had paid off the Bratva, and we hadn't heard from the Russians since. There were always signs that they were still doing some smaller deals with Ford's parents, but I knew they'd never come near us again and it was a peace of mind that I cherished.

True to Ford's promise, although the senior Malones doted on their grandchildren's photos and loaded up their trust funds with regular deposits, they didn't seem terribly interested in *seeing* them much, outside of major holidays or the kids' birthdays.

"I'm just not very good with young children," my mother-in-law had said once, and I hadn't pushed her.

It was perfect, actually. Just the right amount of contact from the Malones.

At one point, they'd indicated to Ford that they were talking to A Guy about divesting from their business. According to my father-in-law, it was, "Just to make things a bit easier for you and the heirs when the time comes."

It seemed to be a tacit admission that Ford's parents were working to sever their Connections, but I didn't try to dig into it any further. Their lives, for the most part, were very separate from ours—and I liked it that way. It allowed all the Zorics/Malones to enjoy every moment of raising this next generation of children without worrying that the shadows of any of their grandparents would ever shade them.

Ford and I opened all the gifts and then, leaving the kids

to play with the piles of wrapping paper, we gathered in the kitchen where Brooklyn was cutting the cake. I sat down and put my feet up. Even after two kids, and now with this third one on the way, I'd never gotten used to how swollen my ankles got. Ford immediately moved behind my chair to rub my shoulders, and I let out a happy sigh.

"Thank you all, for everything," I said.

"It was our pleasure," Brooklyn insisted, passing me the first slice of cake.

"We love you," Tori added.

"I love you too," I said. "All of you."

Once the party had dissipated, with just our family remaining, all of us gathered around the table, eating left-over bits of cake and rocking babies or petting dogs. We'd all done pretty well for ourselves and after the chaos that had come at the start of each of our marriages, we were all now settled into married life. All of us happily.

Truth be told, my brothers were happier than I'd ever seen them. Even though they'd always been protective and caring to me when we were growing up, I had still been surprised by how quickly they had taken to parenthood. Both of them were great fathers. There was no sign they would be anything like the kind of father we'd had.

And Ford continued to amaze me with the amount of love he had for me and the kids. I felt lucky every day.

Brooklyn settled down across from me, while Tori leaned her head on my shoulder, smiling at Stefan who was gathering up the dirty dishes and carrying them to the sink, where Luka was loading everything into the dishwasher. We all had the exhausted parent look on our faces, but we were smiling too. Life was good. Better than good. It was perfect.

I looked around the room, watching the older kids stack

Legos with Ford and the younger ones babble and make messes with their toys. It was chaos, but it was the kind of chaos I liked. I felt at home here, with my family—not just my husband and kids, but with my brothers and sisters and their families. I had a place where I belonged and that was worth more than anything.

"Can you even imagine that one of these days we'll be watching *them* get married?" I asked, trying to envision the little ones all grown up.

Grown up and old enough to get married. It seemed impossible.

I'd asked the question rhetorically, expecting it to be a wistful smiling moment. But of course, Luka came over and answered, still drying his hands on a dish towel. My brother never could resist answering a rhetorical inquiry.

"Yep," he said. "Who do you think will be arranging them?"

Brooklyn smacked him on the arm and I threw a balled-up napkin at him while we all laughed. But as the laughter faded, I could see everyone in the room thinking about it. After all, the point remained. All of our marriages had been arranged in some way.

But by now, we all knew that sometimes, an arrangement was more than a convenience.

More than a sham.

Sometimes, it was the first step to a happy ending.

Ready for a whole new world of delicious alphas and untraditional love stories? Meet the Bellantis, a trio of brothers in wine country, who are trying to cut family ties to the mob after the death of their father.

The saga begins with Broken Bride.

I was sold to him to settle a debt... but Dante Bellanti never settles.

My father was always a gambling man.
Unfortunately, he never could pick winners.
When the wolves closed in, he chose himself, like always.

He traded his freedom... for mine.

He forced me to marry.
Now Dante Bellanti owns my body.
I'm just another possession for a man who already has too much.
So I won't let him have my heart.

But you know what they say about gambling.

The house always wins.

And I'm at the mercy of the Bellantis.

Get Broken Bride here!

PAIGE PRESS

Paige Press isn't just Laurelin Paige anymore...

Laurelin Paige has expanded her publishing company to bring readers even more hot romances.

Sign up for our newsletter to get the latest news about our releases and receive a free book from one of our amazing authors:

Stella Gray
CD Reiss
Jenna Scott
Raven Jayne
JD Hawkins
Poppy Dunne

ALSO BY STELLA GRAY

∼

The Zoric Series

Arranged Series

The Deal

The Secret

The Choice

Convenience Series

The Sham

The Contract

The Ruin

The Convenience Series: Books 1-3

Charade Series

The Lie

The Act

The Truth

∼

The Bellanti Brothers

Dante

Broken Bride

Broken Vow

Broken Trust

ABOUT THE AUTHOR

Stella Gray is an emerging author of contemporary romance. When she is not writing, Stella loves to read, hike, knit and cuddle with her greyhound.

Made in the USA
Monee, IL
12 July 2021

73446450R00132